The Dreaming Girl

*To Nancy,
With best wishes,
Roberta Allen*

by Roberta Allen

The Dreaming Girl
The Traveling Woman
The Daughter
Amazon Dream
Certain People
Fast Fiction

THE DREAMING GIRL

Roberta Allen

Painted Leaf Press
New York City

This is a work of fiction. The characters, incidents, places, dialogues and speeches are products of the author's imagination and are not to be construed as real. The author's use of names of actual persons, living or dead, is incidental to the purposes of the plot and is not intended to change the entirely fictional character of the work.

Copyright ©2000 by Roberta Allen

All rights reserved. Printed in Canada. No part of this book may be used or reproduced in any manner whatsoever without written permission from the publisher except in the case of brief quotations embodied in critical articles and reviews. For information, please address Painted Leaf Press, P.O. Box 2480, Times Square Station, New York, New York 10108-2480.

Cover photo by Roberta Allen
Cover design by Travis Ward
Typesetting by Brian Brunius

The author wishes to thank the Corporation of Yaddo for its hospitality.

Library of Congress Cataloging-in-Publication Data

Allen, Roberta
    The dreaming girl : a novel / by Roberta Allen.
       p. cm.
    ISBN 1-891305-51-4
     I. Title

PS3551.L4157 D74 2000
813'.54–dc21

                                                                   99-089049

To Craig

PART ONE

1

The girl lies on the bed, propped up on her elbows, looking out the window. The window is wide open. The wind blows through the window. The wind blows her long hair. Her hair is like the waves of the sea, undulating in the wind.

The sea crashes on the stones of the promenade outside the window. She is not aware of the window. She is not aware of the room. She is out there with that sea, with that wind, with the sky that hides in the blackness.

She understands the violence in the air. She is part of that violence, part of that blackness. She screams with every bird in her silence. The wind grows stronger, tries to tear the sound from her, but fails. Still, she lets the wind lift her.

From the window, she can fly with those screeching birds. She can sail over the city: this ramshackle city; this city of rag-covered windows and rotting wood, of peeling paint and broken porches, of sagging floors and open sewers, of tattered palms, of heat, of dampness, of rains.

The rains make her mind murky. When it rains, she sails within herself like a boat that has lost direction; she drifts. The rains haven't started yet tonight. But even on the clearest nights, the stars are vague, as though they aren't sure they want to be there.

Tonight there are no stars. She can't even try to grab hold of them. They have taken themselves away from her. The stars are out of reach. But the wind grows strong, so strong it pushes her breaths back inside her; it yanks her hair hard from the scalp.

In the room her hair blows. Nothing else moves in the room. She is still sailing in that sky, but she finds it harder to breathe, harder to catch her breath. Very soon now she will come back. It's inevitable. She can't stay out there for long. Her thoughts get in the way.

As though God has suddenly thrown a bowl of water on the world, rain crashes down, but not straight down. Wind carries the water, throws the water every which way, throws the water in her room; soaks the pillow, part of the sheet before she manages to close the window. She is back now; her face wet, her hair wet, her neck, her shoulders, her chest glisten with water.

She feels robbed by the weather. She would have stayed out there with that sea, with that wind a while longer. She looks around: there is nothing of interest in the room; just the usual walls and floor and ceiling.

The walls don't reach the ceiling in the rooms of the guest house. The walls stop two feet below: there are two feet of open space where in the night, the thoughts, the feelings of the guests circulate and mingle in the air, affecting each other in their sleep without their knowing. They dream of each other, but forget their dreams when they awaken. They awaken with thoughts not their own, with feelings they never knew they had. They breathe each other's breaths, share each other's sorrows.

In the morning when they awaken, they will pass each other without a word. Or if they talk, hello and all that, they will feel suddenly strange, as though they have been stolen, or else they will feel themselves thieves without knowing what it is they have taken.

When the girl awakens, she doesn't remember anything. It is as though she is alive for the very first time. There is the sea smell of the air, the cries of the birds, the blue sky.

She looks up at the blue sky. She goes into that blue like one who is going home, like one who has been in a dark dream and suddenly sees the light. But the light is blinding. She comes back, back to the voices, to the footsteps in the guest house.

Hearing the footsteps makes her remember. This time there is something nice to remember. It was just yesterday that she met him at the guest house. He came in through the screen door, he sat down with her at the table in the common room, this man she calls the German.

She had wanted to meet somebody. It was lonely traveling by herself. Since the last one left her she has been lonely. But now there is the excitement that comes when somebody new enters her life. There is also the fear.

In the shower in the communal bathroom, she forgets about the blue sky and the sea smell of the air. Her eyes are closed while she washes her body. She is dreaming of him as she rubs the bar of soap between her legs.

When she opens the bathroom door, she sees him there in the hallway outside her room. She's wearing a towel which she pulls tighter when she sees him. She doesn't know what to say. She mumbles something. She's embarrassed. She feels as though he knows her dream as she enters her room and closes the door.

While she dresses, the German waits. He hears her moving about, though her room is so small she can only take a few steps in any direction. There is something, something about her, he is thinking. In his mind, he sees the loose hair, almost as long as his hair, the eyes that seem to be the same color as his own. Sympatico, he called her last night.

He is smiling. This was good, this meeting her here like this after his friend had gone on without him.

She opens the door. He's right there. She's surprised to see him so near. There's so little space between them. She needs to take a deep breath, to step back for a minute.

He's smiling at her. It feels good to smile like this. It feels good to show his feelings. He should probably hide his feelings, he knows that, but today he doesn't feel like hiding anything.

The girl is trying to escape his eyes. They're so focused, so directed on her. He's trying to catch her, to hold her with his eyes.

A thought passes through her mind: he wants too much. But so far, he has only asked her to have breakfast. She wants to step back inside the room for a moment just to breathe. She needs air. She feels him taking away her air.

Instead of stepping back inside the room, she follows him down the stairs. She is enjoying herself even though this is a little bit scary. Pale green lizards, sunning themselves on the steps, run and hide in the leaves of the garden. He opens the heavy wooden gate, lets her out, then pushes the latch back into place behind him.

The sun lights up his hair. He turns. The long hair moves with him. The long hair shimmering in the light. For a moment, she thinks of horses; their lean bodies, their smooth skin, their long manes.

He is strange to her. In the bright sunlight, she would like to stare at him. But she doesn't dare. Instead, she stares at clapboard houses they pass along the streets.

They reach the bridge. Twice a day it swings open so tall masted boats may pass through to the sea. Like a huge animal, a strange beast, it moves slowly, making its metallic sounds.

She looks through her camera, tries to find the best angle. He is helpful. "A little farther back," he says, with his heavy accent. "A little to the left. There."

Last night he offered to clean her camera. She had watched his hands; big and rough, the fingers thick, but they moved with such grace, such delicacy. She had wanted to touch them.

She is dreaming about these hands as they enter a restaurant on a small street. They take a table by the window. They look at each other, then look away. They see each other even when they look away.

The sun throws its light on them as they glance out the window. He is smiling again. But this smile is different. He is talking about the world with a sly mocking smile. But even when he smiles this way, the girl feels an openness about his face which makes her want to fly right in, maybe settle there.

The waitress comes over. They order breakfast. They are quiet for a while. When the waitress comes back with their food, the German asks the girl a question. But she doesn't hear.

She is dreaming that she and the German are in the jungle. They are walking down a trail. Amid the trees and vines, they are kissing, they are touching each other. They lie down on the damp earth. He pulls off her pants, parts her legs. She's lying there completely open to him, her knees raised. He lies there, looking. He sees everything. He hasn't touched her yet, but he's about to when the German brings her back with his voice. The light in the restaurant seems very bright to her after the darkness of the jungle. She doesn't quite know where she is.

When he looks at her, he thinks of a necklace breaking. He thinks of beads spilling, rolling, scattering in all directions.

He tries to gather her together with his eyes. "Where are you going next?" he asks.

She wonders if he can look inside her mind and see her dreams. "I want to go to the jungle in the north," she says. "Howler monkeys live there. I want to hear the monkeys roar. People say they roar like jaguars."

He is looking at her. He is trying to figure her out. While he is looking, she absently plays with the dried seahorse in the fishnet that decorates the window. She is wishing he would come with her. But she says nothing. She doesn't know how to say what she wants. She's not used to seeing her dreams happen.

He turns his attention to the room. The room is in shadow as a cloud moves over the sun. He looks down at his empty coffee cup, hears the hum of the fan overhead. He would like to go with her and see the monkeys though he's not sure why.

She looks down at her plate. There are only crumbs now. She rolls the crumbs between her fingers. She gathers the words that are hard to say. She says them over and over in her mind until they lose their meaning. Only then can she get the words out. "You can come with me if you like," she says.

The words don't sound the way she wanted. She is embarrassed. She turns away from the German, stares at the seahorse in the fishnet while he looks at her again.

"I would like to come with you," he says. "If you want, we can leave tomorrow." The girl would like to leave tomorrow. She tells him that, but still she thinks about the words that made her feel embarrassed. Even though the words have produced the result she wanted, she is thinking of different ways she might have said them. Even when the sun comes out from behind the cloud, and fills the room with light, the girl is still embarrassed.

2

He has gone off on his own for the day. She uses this time to think about him, to dream about him. She can be with him even though he is not there.

She is walking down the street, swimming in a dream of him. She is somewhere watery. Flowing. Just his face before her. Large. The body comes later. The body is almost liquid.

Now and then a face outside the dream comes into view. But not for long. It fades like the clapboard houses and the dirty canal and the people standing in the shade, staying out of the way of the sun.

Only the girl walking with her dream takes the sun's heat and light as though they were a gift. As though the sun has given them just to her. The girl walking is large. Her dream makes her large. She is flowing. She is energy and atoms. All the workings of the body seem to show through the skin which is pale.

She is carried along the street by her dream. The dream takes her to the dock, takes her to the boat about to leave for the island. She squeezes between the others, but she doesn't see them. Only the sea and the sky and the dream exist.

The boat boy blows his whistle. White gulls, their wings like knives, cut through the blue sky. The boat flies through the water, past the shacks, past the docks, past the bridge. The sea spread-out is blue-green. Clumps of mangroves rise like strange floating forests.

But soon the wind blurs the sea and the sky and the dream. The wind is still strong when the sun is overhead, and the girl steps off the boat. She walks down the long pier in the wind.

The wind has thrown her off balance. She loses her dream to the wind. She can't even summon the others she keeps in reserve. Without her dreams, the sea and the sky are out of reach. The world is strange when she steps off the pier.

Something is wrong. Like an animal she sniffs it in the air. The other people are gone. She is the last one on shore. She stands alone in the sand. The sand blows. A snake, green and slimy, works its way in the sand. Meat rots in giant conch shells. Shells litter the shore.

There is a street just beyond the sand. A street lined with stilt-legged shacks. Something keeps her from going forward. She doesn't see them yet. But she feels them.

Three Creole men. Their black skins shiny with sweat. Their eyes too bright. They are high. They come toward her. Her heart beats fast. She tells herself to run. But then she stops herself. She doesn't want to show them she is scared. She tries to act normal. The men laugh, come closer, their eyes focused on her. She takes off down a path. "Run, white girl! Run!" they shout, laughing.

She runs down the path by the mangrove swamp. She doesn't stop. She sees nothing but the void of blue sky until up ahead she sees the path end in a little white beach. She turns. No one there. But she keeps on running till she drops to her knees in the sand. She is panting. She lies down. Her arms and legs stretched out, she pretends to be a starfish, she catches her breath as a starfish.

While she lies there stretched out on the sand like a starfish, she looks up at the sky. This is not the sky she wants to see. Right now she yearns for another sky. A Florida sky. The sky above the little house where she grew up.

She closes her eyes. She sees the little house. It's standing there under the Florida sky. But it's not her house anymore. It's not her sky. Her books were still on the shelves when she left. Her clothes were still in the closet. Her mother said, 'If you leave now, you can never come back!'

She is twenty-one. She is never going back. Not to the house, nor to the bar where she worked as a barmaid. She doesn't have to. Her aunt left her money. If she is careful, she can live on that money for three or four years. She hears her mother screaming, 'You are crazy!' Then she hears herself screaming at her mother. She is screaming that she wants to see the world.

While she hears the screaming voices of her mother and herself, the mosquitoes come. So many mosquitoes! They are biting her all over. She forgets her mother, the little house, the Florida sky. She looks at the water. She strips to her swim suit, runs to the water.

The water is soft and warm. She is floating. Her body feels elastic following the motion of little rippling waves. She moves with the water, moves without a will; lets the water have its way with her. She abandons herself to this sea.

She has let the current pull her too far out. She is a dot in a wide expanse of blue-green sea. The palms look like toys when she opens her eyes and sees them from a distance. She has awakened from her dream of water.

Her arms and legs move against the current in a rhythm of their own. The silvery barracudas, the schools of little striped fish take note of her passing. The body is like a motor now, streamlined and stroking, the mouth blowing out air. When the girl with the motor-like body reaches the shore, she is breathless and pale.

She lies there on the sand, her eyes closed. She doesn't see the white speedboat pulling in to shore. The man in the boat, a Mayan, is looking for tourists to take to the reef. He is a short man, thick and muscular. Surly. He calls out to her. "Do you want to see the reef?"

She opens her eyes, she looks at him, she finds him handsome. "I don't have money," she says. "You must have some money," he says. "How much do you have in there?" he asks, pointing to her backpack on the sand. She reaches over, looks through it, pulls out some crumpled bills. "That's enough," he tells her.

She looks at him, she hesitates. Then she decides what to do. She doesn't want to be alone on this island. She goes over, she hands him the bills.

Only when she steps into the boat does she see the tiny dagger piercing his ear. The dagger makes her nervous. Maybe she shouldn't go. Maybe she should say she changed her mind. But she is too afraid to say anything until the boat heads out toward the reef. "No," she says, suddenly. "I want to see the mangrove swamps." She thinks she will be safer if they stay near shore.

He turns the boat, cuts the motor, enters a lagoon, dark and still. Mosquitoes cover their faces, their arms, their legs. Her hands fly up over her face. He backs the boat out into the sea, opens the engine. The boat leaps ahead at full speed. The water and the sky blur. The girl likes the speed of the boat. "Don't stop!" she says.

As long as the boat keeps moving, she isn't afraid. "You don't want to see the reef?" he asks her. "No," the girl says. "I want to go around the island." The Mayan looks at her. His eyes are mocking, amused.

She feels his eyes as she looks up at the sky, squinting. The bright sun has drained the sky of color. But the reef looks deep purple in the blue-green sea. She looks out at the sea. At first, she tries to forget the Mayan. But then she gives in, she lets herself dream.

The girl in the dream is not shy like the dreamer. She doesn't look away when she feels his eyes. In the dream, she slips off the straps of her swim suit. She looks at him, her breasts bare. Then she slips the suit over the rest of her body. She opens her legs wide, rubs her hand between her thighs.

In the dream, the Mayan stops the boat in the shallow water of the reef. He comes over to her, opens his pants, lets it out.

She looks at it. It is thick and pulsing. She slides her tongue along the side of it. Then she takes it in her mouth, feels the fullness of him in her mouth.

In the moment when she feels the fullness of him, she hears the hum of insects; the same low hum she heard in the dark chambers of Mayan ruins as she wandered through temples and tombs. These were the sounds of wasps locked within the Mayan walls. She hears these sounds while stroking him with her tongue, while circling the tip.

All the time she is stroking him, she is looking at his body. She doesn't stop looking. She takes in the smoothness of the skin, its warm brown color in contrast to his open white shirt flapping in the wind. While she is stroking him, she listens to the wind and the humming insects deep within the Mayan walls. The wasps are fanning the nests with their wingbeats.

As she continues to stroke him with her tongue, the hum of insects grows louder. The wasps are agitated; flying, crawling over each other excitedly. She uses her hands now as well as her mouth to bring him to that final release. But the humming insects are so loud she doesn't hear him cry out.

His voice wakes her from the dream. "Have you had enough?" the Mayan asks. He looks bored. He's been going in circles for almost an hour. "Yes," the girl says.

3

It's evening. The girl is waiting for the German at the guest house. She is sitting upstairs at the table in the common room. The walls are dark and stained. The maps hanging on the walls are faded. She looks at her watch.

She is sorry she didn't go with the German to the ruins. If she were with him now, she wouldn't be waiting. She would be having an adventure. The German didn't know if he could reach the ruins. The bus stops far away on the road. Between the road and the ruins, there is nothing but jungle, he said.

While she waits, she tries to distract herself by looking through her guidebook. But she sees nothing. Just lines on the page. Not even words. Not even letters. Just lines.

She goes downstairs, buys a soda. Just to do something. There is an odd looking woman with gray braids at the desk. There is a knife on the desk. The girl looks at it. "Is that a machete?" she asks. The woman nods, tells her it's for the crackheads. She says one came through the door last night. "The locked door! Nothing stops them," she says.

The girl goes back upstairs. She thinks about the German in the jungle. Maybe she is lucky that she didn't go with him. What if he never comes back? What if he's been bitten by a snake, or a scorpion? What if he's fallen, twisted his ankle on a vine?

His mother will wonder why he never came back. His mother and all the people in the little German village where he lives. Months from now they will still wonder. They will picture him—his mother especially—in a hot country with jungle.

Or maybe they won't know what to picture. Maybe they won't even know the country where he is lost. Could be one of several countries. Who will know? Who will give them the details?

The mother will wait a long time before she will make inquiries. She will wait until she is sure he is dead. Then she will learn about the girl. She will write her a letter or call her on the telephone.

In her heavy accent, she will say: 'I heard you knew my son.' Her only son, her only child. But the girl won't have much to tell. 'I didn't know him very well,' she will say. 'We were supposed to meet for dinner, but he never came back.'

She is surprised when the German opens the screen door. He is not supposed to be here. His fate is mysterious. Tragic. She is telling his mother the little she knows. She tells her with tearful eyes.

But now she will have to dry her eyes. She will have to say goodbye to his mother. The connection between them is broken. By appearing at the door, he has cut the girl off from his family, from his friends, from the little German village where he lives.

He is so pleased to see her he doesn't notice the tears in the corners of her eyes.

She looks at him and sees a man who has returned from the dead. He looks better than ever. He looks better than the German she dreamed, even though he is dirty, his shirt torn, his boots and pants caked with mud. He looks so good the girl wants to pinch him to make sure that he is real. But she doesn't have to pinch him. She feels his hand on her shoulder.

He sits down beside her. He is taking off his shirt. He is doing it without thinking. She thinks he is taking it off because it is dirty and torn. But he is doing it because he wants to show off his beautiful body. There is no better place to show off his body than in a hot tropical country. Here, he can take off his shirt and it seems natural, it seems normal. No one knows that he is showing off.

The girl is blushing. He likes that. There is something old-fashioned about a girl who can blush. She tries to admire him the way she would admire a beautiful vase or a beautiful statue. But he moves and breathes. He is alive. "What happened?" she asks him. Her heart beats fast.

He looks at his muddy pants. "As you can see, I was walking in the jungle," he says, laughing. The moment he talks about the trip it plays like a film in his mind. He only tells her parts of it, but he sees the film uncut.

While he talks, the girl looks at his eyes, his mouth. But the German sees only his trip.

On the bus he is smiling. He can't help himself. He is thinking about his life three months ago. He was working in a printing plant in Germany. He was longing for adventure. He feels as though three years have passed.

But then the bus stops. He is disappointed. He sees the dirt road to the ruins, wide enough for a car. The dirt road is too easy. He had pictured himself climbing over vines, tearing through branches and leaves.

He is sorry he listened to the travelers who told him about the ruins. The trail from the highway was overgrown, impossible to find, they said. Even if he found it, his worries would not be over. There were snakes and jaguars and clouds of mosquitoes and biting flies.

He is walking along the dirt road, kicking stones on the path. This is not his idea of an adventure. But then he starts looking through the trees, covered with moss and vines and lichen. He is suddenly a small boy. He is looking for a secret trail through the jungle to the ruins.

The small boy stops and listens to the insects and the birds. At first, he doesn't hear the silence. But the silence is all around him. The silence is thick and heavy. It is something he can almost touch.

He walks on. The jungle seems to hold itself back from him. It seems to hide in its darkness. He is no longer the small boy. The darkness of the jungle is not his darkness. His darkness is deep inside him. He sees only what the jungle lets him see. He knows there is more. The small boy would have seen more. But the small boy is hiding in his darkness.

In the silence, thoughts and feelings the German tries to bury come out of his darkness into the light of day. In the silence, he can hear his mother saying, 'You are just like your father. When he was young he was handsome too. He couldn't stay still just like you. He was always running off. If you don't watch out, you'll end up just like him!' He sees his father. His big belly. He is drunk. He sees his father's wife. The blond hair. The red lips. He sees the three of them standing in the yard. There are weeds, beer cans, garbage. His father's wife is laughing, patting him on the head. He is only a boy. He is confused.

The loud froglike croak of a toucan brings him back to the dirt path. Up ahead, he sees a clearing and a huge stone ruin rising high above the earth. On the stones of the temple, he sees the marks of war, of weather, of time. In the silence, he climbs the long steep stairs to the top. He looks out over the plaza. There are more temples, palaces, mounds still covered by jungle. Green parakeets streak by. Mockingbirds and brown jays squawk.

He is alone in the ancient city; alone in this place so violently abandoned though no one knows why. In the silence, he thinks about the girl in the guest house. He thinks of her long hair. He thinks about the way she looks at him out of the corner of her eye. He forgets the silence. He even forgets the feeling that he is being watched. Are there spirits watching? Are there ghosts?

He is still thinking about the girl when suddenly he sees a tarantula on the stone platform where he is standing. He forgets the girl. The small boy comes alive. The tarantula is dead, is decomposing, but the small boy doesn't mind. He bends down to see it better. He pokes it with a stick. He looks at it until there is nothing more to see. Then he runs up and down the stairs of temples and palaces. He wanders through archways and chambers.

When he tires of the ruins, the small boy finds a secret trail in the jungle. He walks through tangled roots and vines and leaves. He climbs over fallen trees, sunk in mud. He comes to a pond, fed by springs and rain. Here are fish and lizards and frogs and turtles and snakes.

He follows the trail beyond the pond. He stops now and then to look at columns of ants, butterflies with see-through wings, vines coiled like corkscrews. At times, he is knee-deep in mud. He chases clouds of mosquitoes from his face. The trees around him drip with slime. Thorns scratch his skin, rip his shirt. He is happy. This is what he calls an adventure until he comes to a place with trees and vines and roots so thick and tangled he has to turn back.

By the time he reaches the empty highway, he is no longer the small boy. The German stands there in the sun, looking, listening for the sound of a car, a bus. After a while, he is tired of looking, tired of listening. He lets his mind drift. He sees the house where he lives. An old house. Run-down. It is hidden in the woods, a few miles from a little German village. He can see people in the village shake their heads at the sight of his banged-up car. He can hear them laugh when they see the ring in his girlfriend's nose. He can see parties they gave for their friends in the yard, the weeds so tall they almost hide the outhouse.

The hours pass. The sky is dark. The house feels further and further away, as he stands there on the empty highway. It feels as though he has never lived in that house. It feels as though that house isn't real. Nothing is real but the road and the silence. He closes his eyes; he tries to see his girlfriend. But even with his eyes closed, the darkness of the sky seeps into his mind. Before he sees her clearly, she fades into the darkness.

At last, he hears the bus. He sees the headlights. He goes out on the highway. He is shouting, waving his arms. But the bus goes past, without stopping.

He is still cursing, stamping his feet when he sees more lights. A truck is coming. He cries out. The truck stops. He climbs in back, sits down beside some farmers.

"I was lucky," he says to the girl. "I could have waited there all night." He has come to the end of the film in his mind. He stops talking.

He has told her about the temples and palaces. He has told her about the trail in the jungle. But he hasn't told her about the silence of the ruins or the darkness inside him. He hasn't told her about the small boy.

He's not sure he understands the silence, the darkness, the small boy. He doesn't know how to talk about things he doesn't understand.

He is tired now. His eyes close. He drifts off for a moment, then wakes up to find the girl still looking at him. She feels as though she knows him, but she only knows her dream.

If she didn't have her dream of the German, she would lose herself: she would be like water in his hands. Better to lose herself in a dream than to lose herself in a man.

The dream is safe. The German in the dream is only the way that she dreams him. He will never surprise her like the German sitting here now.

She jumps when he touches her hand. She didn't expect him to do that. She doesn't know how to be with him when he does something that she doesn't expect even if that something shows that he cares, even if that something proves that he wants her.

She wants him to be the way that she dreams him: she wants to see him do and say the things that are familiar from her dream. It is scary for her to see that he lives a life apart from the one she dreams.

He only touched her hand to see her ring. He is looking at the stone. "Jade?" he says.

That night, sleeping in her bed alone, she dreams of little jade figures. The little figures are walking down a path that goes around the world. The world is spinning while they are walking. Sometimes they are walking at the top of the world. Sometimes they are walking on the bottom. She wonders why they don't fall off.

Early in the morning, the girl and the German are walking down the street with their duffels. They are going for breakfast to a Chinese place that opens before the others. They go in and sit down. The place is crowded with Creole people.

The girl and the German shoo the flies away. But the flies come back. When the eggs are served, more flies come. The girl continues to wave the flies away with her hand. But the German ignores them.

The German is very quiet. He is thinking. There is something he needs to say. He doesn't want to say it. If it wasn't forcing itself to be said, he wouldn't tell her.

But it keeps forcing itself on him, so he has to get it out. "I have a girlfriend back home," he says.

She looks at him. She is disappointed. She is surprised. But the girlfriend doesn't change her dream. The German in her dream will be there with her long after this German is gone.

She asks about the girlfriend. She doesn't want to know, but she wants to tell him in her way that it's all right. Even though it isn't all right.

When he sees the smile that masks her disappointment, he thinks he did the right thing by telling her. As they walk to the bus that goes to the jungle, his steps are those of a man without a care.

A little blue school bus, an old bus from the States, stands on the corner of a street with houses that look drunk. The houses may fall down at any moment. Steps are missing from the stairs. The sun beats down on the rusty roofs.

Children yell. Men and boys ride by on bicycles. There are no other whites. Only them. The German feels uneasy. But the girl doesn't mind. She likes to look in people's houses. Even when there is nothing to see. Even when it is dark inside. And she can see only the corner of a table. Or a curtain pulled back. Or a plastic pitcher. These are traces of people's lives. She likes to see how people live. People who are not like her.

The German is interested in the way she looks at people on the street or at their windows. She has a very direct way of looking at people she doesn't know.

The bus isn't leaving yet. So they have time to look. They have time to let themselves be seen. It's too hot to wait inside the bus so they stand on the street, walk around.

The blacks don't like them being here. The blacks tell them with their eyes that this is not the part of town where they belong. But this is the only place where the bus stops that goes up north to the jungle where the howler monkeys roar.

The black people slowly board the bus. The little girls wear starched dresses. Their hair is braided with ribbons. They sit up straight like little dolls while old ladies fuss over their dresses, their hair. They fuss even though the air is as hot as an oven.

The old ladies and the old men, some with cardboard boxes, speak Creole. The black people laugh and talk among themselves. The girl and the German don't understand what is said.

The blacks pay no attention to the whites. Only the bus driver gives them a nod. They feel very white on this bus. They feel left out from all the fun. Being poor doesn't stop the blacks from having fun. Being hot doesn't stop them either.

The bus rolls along the bumpy road. Dust fills the air. The girl and the German look out the windows and see the dust, feel the dust in their eyes. Even without the dust, there would be nothing to see. Just road. Some trees. Some sky.

In the bus, the blacks grow more lively. Everyone is laughing, even the ones hidden behind their cardboard boxes.

The girl and the German look at each other. They smile. They look away. Like a barrier their duffels rest between them on the seat. But in the moments when their eyes meet, they seem to be infected by the laughter of the blacks: the barriers between them disappear.

Now and then one of them points out a river or a bridge or a bird.

The seats bounce on the bumpy road. The girl laughs as she bounces on the seat. There is nothing like the bumpy road and the excitement of moving. When she looks over at the German, she sees in his face that he feels the excitement too.

She feels almost cocky when she asks to see a picture of his girlfriend. He takes one out. She is blond, pretty. But she is only a picture. Pictures don't count. What matters is the fact that they are moving. They are going forward into the unknown.

They look out the window. There is jungle all around them now. A river shows itself from time to time. But mostly there is jungle, thick and green. They can't see anything through the wall of green. Then suddenly a village comes into view.

4

The bus lets them off. They look around. This is the center of the village: a couple of bars, two or three stores. Up the road are green fields on either side and barbed wire fences. There are fruit trees. There are little farm houses scattered over the fields. The houses shimmer in the heat. The sky is large.

Where the fields stop, the jungle begins. The jungle surrounds the fields, surrounds the village. There is also a river, the one they saw from the bus; a fast brown river that cuts through the jungle, but the girl and the German can't see it from where they stand.

Some chickens cross the road. This doesn't look like a place where howler monkeys roar. This poor plain village. But the girl and the German are not disappointed.

They have seen houses and fields and jungles before, but nowhere else can they see exactly what they see now. Nowhere else would this blue house stand out in the green pasture. Nowhere else would the shadow of this white cloud darken the small patch of field to this exact shade of green.

It is not so much what they are seeing that excites them: it is the way they are seeing. They are seeing the village through the excitement they have carried over from the bus ride. They see with fresh eyes. At this moment, everything they see is new.

A fat black woman in a loose dress stands outside her store, hands on hips. The German asks her where they can rent a room. She points up the road, then turns to a boy, and tells him to show them the way.

The boy goes on ahead. The girl and the German follow. They are new. Untried. Like children. They walk up the road, cross a field, climb through barbed wire. The jungle stands back, pushed there by the fields. But the fields can't keep away the sounds.

Unearthly sounds drift through the air from the jungle. The girl and the German stop and listen. They look at each other. They've never heard roars like this. Only the boy goes on, as though he doesn't hear.

When they begin, the monkeys' roars remind the girl of grating metal chains. But then a sadness enters the sounds. The raspy roar becomes a wail. The wailing is so loud the girl and the German hold their ears. Soon the wailing turns into a chorus of anguished moans. These sounds of sorrow and suffering are enough to break the heart.

The roars of the howler monkeys change the way they see the village. They can't see the village now apart from this sadness, this sorrow hanging over it. Even when the monkeys are still, the sadness and sorrow are there.

The boy waits for them at the green house that was pale green once. Now it is a dirty color. An old woman, very tall, her head high, stands by the door. "Do you want one room or two?" she asks.

The German's face goes blank. He doesn't want to be the one who decides. He leaves it in her hands. He doesn't know what else to do.

The girl says, "We want two rooms." She thinks this will please him. But she can't tell by his face if he is pleased or not.

The old woman leads the German to the room by the kitchen. The girl follows. The little room, with a bare bulb, and walls made of cinderblocks, is hot like an oven. The windows are unscreened. But the German doesn't seem to mind. He throws down his duffel on the large bed.

The girl is led to the room next door. This room is smaller and hotter than his room. But she keeps her displeasure to herself.

The old woman brings her a tin pail so she won't have to use the outhouse at night. The outhouse is far away in the field. The shower is far away too. The old woman takes them to see the shower; a three-walled tin shed with nothing inside.

At the back of the house, the old woman keeps pails filled with rain water. "Let me know when you want to bathe, Miss," the old woman says. She will bring a pail to the shed, and douse her with rain water.

The girl goes back to her room. She stands in it, looks around. She doesn't want to stay here. She wants to stay with him. But she doesn't know how to tell him. She walks outside, tries to work up the courage, tries to find the right words.

If she were somebody else, she could find the courage. Somebody else wouldn't be afraid. Sometimes, when she dreams she is somebody else, she can do things she can't do as herself. When she goes next door to see the German, somebody else is going in her place.

Even as somebody else she can't tell him what she wants, at least not directly. But he gets the hint when she complains about her room. "You can stay with me," he says, as though nothing could be more natural. The girl looks at him. She is surprised.

The German would like to be the kind of man who can say what he just said. He would like to be able to take life as it comes. But he is not that kind of man. Even while he told her that she can stay with him, he saw the girlfriend in his mind. How can I let her stay in that awful room? he said to the girlfriend who isn't there.

He asks the girl to rest a while with him. He lies down across the bed. He tries to forget about the girlfriend. The girl lies down beside him. Their bodies sink into the soft mattress. They lie there without touching, listening to the sounds. The monkeys start up again. They hear the sadness, the sorrow. But right where they are, where their eyes meet, a seed has taken root; the seed grows while the sounds try to distract them; it grows while the dogs bark, the chickens squawk, the children yell; it grows while the elders scold the children, scold the dogs.

The seed growing between them isn't growing fast enough for the girl. She is impatient. While they lie on the bed, without touching, without speaking, the girl's impatience fills the room. He feels her impatience. It makes him nervous. He suggests they walk down to the river.

The old woman sees them cross the field. She calls out, "Don't go far! Dinner will be ready soon." They turn and smile. Then they continue down the road. From the road, they take a little path. They vanish through the trees.

They see the river in the fading light. Clouds move in the sky. The clouds turn pink and orange and violet. The colors dance on the water. Mist hangs between the water and the sky. The trees are turning dark.

As the light dies, the world gets smaller. The world is

manageable now in the light that is left. The world is small enough to fit inside their eyes. The girl and the German say nothing. They take in the water and the sky. How easy it is to stand there; wanting nothing, needing nothing. For a little while, the dying world of the day offers itself to them.

Then the world of the night is born. Insects take over, forcing them to go. They walk back up the road in the dark. They watch the stars come out in the sky. The sky is large. So large.

They are laughing. Dancing. They are part of this great black space. Everything is so big and open now. The cows rest. The fields are so wide. They are dancing through the fields in the dark, moving toward the electric light in the kitchen of the green house.

The old woman waits for the whites in the doorway of the kitchen. She hears their laughter. In the jungle, the monkeys make their terrible music, but the girl and the German dance to music of their own.

In the kitchen the children wait for them. They jump up and down. The beauty is six. Her sister is seven. Their little brother is four. They are curious, so curious about the whites.

When the girl and the German sit down at the table, the children laugh and touch their strange white skins. They pinch them. They pull the hairs on their arms. Round and round the table they run, screaming. "Stop that!" the old woman, their grandmother, shouts.

The girl laughs. The German laughs too. The beauty comes over and stares into her face. The beauty smiles. She is a little bit in love with the white girl's face. The beauty touches her pale skin, her long loose hair. The beauty giggles. Then she sways and sucks her thumb. "Come over here!" the old woman yells at the beauty. "Let them eat in peace!"

Three dogs with big sad eyes wait for food by their feet. The dogs yelp. "Shoo! Shoo!" says the old woman to the dogs. Mosquitoes and flies circle the light. The girl and the German slap the insects on their arms, their faces, while they eat rice and beans and chicken. They tell the old woman the food is very good. She smiles at them a smile just for tourists.

She waits for them to finish: she waits to feed her family. Her husband comes downstairs, looks them over. He hates white people. They see that. But he says, "Hello." What else can he do? They say hello back.

When they step outside, there are so many insects they run to the room. But the room is no better. Insects come through the windows. It's too hot to shut the wooden blinds. The German stops the girl from turning on the light. He has a candle. He says the candle won't attract so many bugs.

But still the bugs come. The girl keeps slapping her arms, her neck, her face. The German squishes the bugs between his fingers. He goes after one, then another. He can't stop.

Maybe if he kills all the insects in the room he will know what to do about the girl. He feels his girlfriend watching. He is only killing insects, he says to the girlfriend who isn't there.

The girl is sitting on the edge of the bed, waiting. He feels her eyes. He tries not to think about her. He tries to cast her from his mind the way he cast from his mind the other girls he met. But it was easier with the others. He didn't feel anything.

In every town, in every village, there was always a girl who took his hand and placed it on her breast, or between her legs. But every time he said no. He is tired of saying no. He's been too long without a woman.

He thinks to himself this is stupid. He'll never kill all the insects. He stops. Just like that. There is a question in her eyes. But he pretends not to notice.

From his duffel, he pulls out a tape player. Then he pulls out some tapes. He asks if she likes Celia Cruz. "Who?" she says.

Lying down on the bed, he tells her to listen, and turns on the tape. She lies down beside him. They listen to the songs; look up at the ceiling, see the shadows from the flame.

He tells her all about Celia Cruz. He loves her songs. The girl doesn't care for the singer, but she likes to watch his face while he is talking; she likes to see it change. The brows come together, fly apart. The mouth slackens for a moment. She likes to look at him, but she grows sleepy. Her eyes close.

She is dreaming as he pulls her to him. She is dreaming this body pressed against hers. She is dreaming the real body. But the body is no longer real because she is dreaming it. The body is no longer made of muscle and bone. Blood is not rushing through this body. This body can't be bruised or broken.

Her hands move down his body. She is touching skin, but this skin is not his skin except for that moment when she sees through a rip in the dream, the otherness of his body. At that moment, she breathes in his scent, listens to his heart beat, feels the moistness of his lips.

But she is too afraid to let the dream and the body be one, so she is learning a body that is not his body. She is learning the body of the dream. She goes step by step, testing, trying things out.

The German moans while she gives him pleasure. But she hears only the German in her dream.

Part Two

1

In the room in the green house, the girl and the German sleep. Outside is the grassy field. Beyond the field is the jungle. The jungle surrounds their sleep. The jungle lives at the borders of their sleep.

The jungle is black in the night. Blacker than the sky. Blacker than anything the girl has seen. The girl sees the blackness in a dream. She dreams the blackness. The jungle is too black to see without the dream.

While the German sleeps the girl enters the blackness, enters the dream. The blackness is alive. The girl can feel the life in the blackness. The jungle is big and black and alive. She makes her way through the blackness.

The German's sleep is smooth and sleek as polished stone. There's no place for the girl or the dream in his sleep. From deep inside the dream, she looks out and sees the German sleeping. He is far away, she is thinking. But she is not alone in the dream.

She sees millipedes, and beetle larvae crunching through the solid wood of trees. She sees termites running around their large boil-like nests on the tree trunks. She sees fungi fruiting on the corpses of moths and spiders and giant ants.

In a heap of dung, she sees metallic flies flap their wings and charge one another. She sees beetles, ripe with eggs, feeding. She sees other beetles drag great loads of dung to a hole the female has made. She watches the female carry the dung inside to feed her larvae. She sees males with long rhinoceros-like horns fight fiercely over females and dung. She sees long sleek beetles burrow under the dung for smaller beetles, fly larvae, insect eggs. She sees stingless bees carry dung in pockets on their legs to bring back to their nests.

She sees ants and butterflies feed on bird droppings. She sees large bats search for birds and lizards to bring home to their roosts in hollow trees. By the trees, she sees a profusion of feathers. The remains of their victims she sees lying in the roost holes which are covered with bones, dried blood, and droppings. She sees the holes seething with insect larvae and full grown beetles.

She watches a sloth hang upside down from a limb, high in a tree. She sees the algae growing in its fur. Down below, she sees spiders catching small birds in their sticky nets. She sees the sap of a fallen tree attract clouds of noisy fruit flies.

She sees mosses, ferns, orchids, bromeliads, cacti. She sees thick layers of lichen, algae, and mosses wrap themselves around the trees. She sees ferns growing on mosses, orchids on ferns, pineapples on lichens. She sees vines snaking their way upward or sprawling across the forest floor.

She sees parrots and long-tailed macaws feeding on a fruiting fig tree. In the same tree, she sees monkeys greedily devour the figs. She sees peccaries and pacas and agoutis feed on the fruit which have fallen to the earth while above them, she sees geckos, bobbing their heads and flicking their white-tipped tails, as they defend their territory on the tree trunk.

She sees scorpions lunge from narrow crevices in the fig tree, seizing cockroaches and crickets, while on the forest floor, she sees land snails leave slick mucous trails, she sees frogs cram earthworms into their mouths with their hands, she sees caterpillars eat one another.

She sees an ant queen tear, bite, and rub off her wings after mating in the air. She watches hordes of voracious ants eat slow-moving snakes, gorged with food. She sees other ants inject venomous stings into nestling birds and sleeping frogs. She watches as they carve the creatures into movable chunks.

She sees a multitude of amorous frogs suddenly appear in a newly formed pool, eager to lay their eggs where there are no fish to threaten their young. She hears the din of screeching frogs in the heat of mating.

She sees a pair of disembodied eyes that look like hot orange coals. The eyes belong to a honey bear high in a tree. She sees the honey bear look down on green soupy water, where crocodile eyes glow bright orange in the night. She sees an egret eat a young crocodile while other young crocodiles eat water bugs.

She sees fleas burrow under the skin of a rat. She hears the sharp barks of the rat echo in the blackness. She sees other rats, with flea eggs growing and swelling in their blood: in some, she sees eggs the size of peas, bursting with larvae.

She sees venom smelling like excrement ooze from the glands of millipedes while mosquitoes suck the blood of birds. She sees butterfly larvae, punctured by the sticky hairs of the passionflower, bleed to death as they starve.

On the forest floor, she sees the female scorpion devour the male after mating. She watches a scorpion nearby seize a spider and tear it to bits, while young scorpions ride around on their mother's back.

She sees a fly straddling a butterfly while devouring it. She sees a beetle follow a snail into its shell, biting it and squirting a fluid until the snail is overcome. She sees the female mantis bite off the head of the male while mating.

In a burrow under a tree, she sees young iguanas fight their way out of rubbery eggs. By a pool, she smells the foul musk of turtles, and sees iguanas eat the worm-infested dung of other iguanas. She watches a mantis catch a lizard, and eat it alive. She sees a male tapir sniff a female's urine before they mate. With their long narrow tongues, she sees honey bears lick out the honey in bees' nests.

She sees a puma break a deer's neck by quickly pulling its head to the side. She hears mating pumas scream, their lips curled back, their teeth bared. By a spine-covered tree, she sees a male puma killing its young.

She hears peccaries squeal and grunt as their malodorous scent floats through the forest. She watches an anteater's sharp claws tear open a termite nest and trap the insects with its sticky saliva. She sees an armadillo burrow into a dead snake to get at the maggots.

In a wasp nest, she sees the queen wasp destroying the eggs of the lesser queens. She sees other wasps chew pieces of caterpillar to feed the larvae. She sees blind naked black-skinned chicks emerge from antbird eggs in a tree nearby.

She sees a small viper, coiled, in a thicket of heliconia. She sees a hummingbird come along, attracted by the large red flowers. She watches the viper strike with its fangs.

She sees a giant toad squirt poison from its glands, and two male frogs, arms wrapped around each other, heads thrown back, wrestle on the forest floor. She watches another frog pull off its skin and swallow it, while howler monkeys roar.

All this the girl sees in the dream as she makes her way through the blackness. At first, she feels only the horror and the slime of life. She feels it in her mouth, on her hands, on her skin, in her bowels, on the soles of her feet. But even as she feels the horror and the slime, she sees herself outside of life. She sees herself apart from all the other living things. She makes her way through the jungle, through the blackness without being part of the life and death around her in the dream.

But as she watches all the other living things in the blackness, the horror she feels gives way to wonder. She sees in the dream that she is alive like all the other living things. Watching the life around her isn't enough. She wants to be part of it. She dives into the blackness to be with the other living things. Once she dives into the blackness, she's not outside of life anymore. There is no one watching. There is no one dreaming. There is only the jungle and the blackness. The dream is no longer a dream.

She has broken through to the other side. The other side of the dream is life. She's inside of life now like the other living things. There's no horror here. Life is beyond horror, nightmare, dream, beauty, wonder. But she can only be in life for a little while. After a while, she goes off. She needs something less real. The going off is inevitable. She goes back inside the dream.

But even after she is back inside the dream, there is a knowing in the skin, in the body. The knowing is not something to talk about, discuss, or even think about.

The knowing is something that life leaves. It is an invisible mark, an invisible stain. It is the silence in the heart of a sound.

This knowing is the feeling that leaves have when they are touched by the sun. It is the feeling of flying things when they are flying, crawling things when they are crawling, swimming things when they are swimming. It is the feeling that plants have when they shoot from the earth to reach for the stars.

This knowing opens the leaves, the buds, makes the petals fall from flowers. All the living things that burrow in the earth, that hide in the trees know life. This is what the trembling leaves know when the branches sway.

As she walks again in the dream, the leaves touch her with their knowing, the roots touch her, the vines touch her. There is life touching life. The living things that land on her body know her body is land like the earth.

In the dream, she listens to the sounds that life makes: the sounds of knowing; the constant hum, the chatter, the cries, the songs, the clicks, the squeals, the whimpers, the grunts. There are splashes, the flutter of wings, the breathing in, the breathing out.

She is breathing in, breathing out. She is coming up from deep inside the dream. She is waking from the dream of the jungle to the dream of the room in the green house. The German lives in this dream. He lies beside her on the bed. He is stretching. The light is starting. The light is thin and watery and purple. The light is like a faint stain in the air. It's too soon to see the white glow of the sun.

Pushing the hair from their eyes and stretching takes all their attention. Before the sounds of the day can be heard, the voices of sleep must be still. The light casts its faint purplish glow on their bodies. The sheet is pushed aside. The wrinkled sheet. The sheet he brought from home to comfort him in strange beds.

She can't tell where he leaves off and she begins. She is touching skin that could be his or hers. The skin could even be the sheet. The sheet is soft and damp like their bodies.

He was awake. But now he sleeps again. He is lying on his side, dreaming. She can tell by the way his lips move slightly. He is a dream dreaming. She tries to imagine his dream as she stares at his face.

Slowly, he wakes up again. He pulls her down on top of him. He fits so perfectly inside her. It makes her feel that she must be empty when he's not there. She is lost in the dream of him. She sighs, her head back, her eyes closed. She surrounds him with her heat as she sails through the sky like the light from a comet. Afterwards they cover themselves with the sheet. They sleep again. They go into the great nowhere.

They are brought back by the sounds of the day. The dogs bark. The chickens squawk. There are roosters. There are the loud froglike croaks of toucans. The low-pitched calls of motmots. The chatter of swallows. The loud back and forth calling of antbirds. In the distance, the monkeys roar. But loudest of all are the children.

The beauty, her sister, and the little brother come to the windows, see them lying under the sheet. They scream with excitement, jump up and down. They think they have caught them in the act. The beauty dances round, laughing, staring at their white toes sticking out beneath the sheet.

The girl and the German are laughing. They find it funny that the children are standing there, watching them. They find it funny because they are happy. The old woman, their grandmother, doesn't find it funny. "Get away from there!" she yells.

2

The girl and the German want to see the monkeys. The old woman says they shouldn't go into the jungle alone. Her husband will take them. The old man doesn't look happy. But he does what he is told.

The girl and the German follow him across the field, crawl through barbed wire fences. Suddenly they find themselves in jungle. It is warm and dark and damp. The trail is hard to see between the trees. The old man and the German walk faster than the girl. The girl can't see them now. All she sees are the leaves and the vines and the trees.

It is dark. Very dark. The trees block out the light. But in the darkness, she is not afraid. The darkness is like the darkness of the dream. She spreads out in the darkness like spilled liquid. Her edges melt away.

She is there with the plants pushing through the earth. She is there with the trees stretching toward the light. She is there with the oozing slime, the glistening eggs, the decomposing bodies. She is there with the ants devouring birds newly hatched, bite by bite. She is there with the frogs, their mouths full of bugs. She is not yet fixed, not yet hardened: she is raw life waiting to be formed.

From far off, she hears his voice calling. She doesn't want to leave this darkness which is more than a dream. But already it is too late. His voice has broken the spell.

When she catches up to him, he points out three monkeys in the branches of a tree. There is excitement on his face. The excitement of the small boy. The small boy is full of wonder.

The German as a small boy is someone new to the girl. She's not sure who to be with this boy. The small boy isn't part of her dream. She can't connect the small boy with what she knows of the German. She can't pin him down. He doesn't stay still. He runs around the tree to see the monkeys from all angles.

She looks at the monkeys too. But she isn't thinking about monkeys. She is thinking about the German. If only he would be more like her dream. She doesn't know what to expect from him now. She doesn't know who he is. He is impenetrable like a house closed for the winter. She is locked out. Her dream can't open his door. Her dream can only give her entry to her own house.

Above them in the trees, the male monkey lets loose the terrible roars. She forgets her thoughts. She looks at the monkey's mouth. The open mouth. The mouth big enough to swallow the world.

She sees herself and the German inside the great black cave of the monkey's mouth. She feels the darkness, the dampness. The walls are wet and smooth. The stones are slippery. He takes her hand. They step from stone to stone, without knowing where their steps will lead them. A fetid smell hangs in the air. There is running water somewhere. There are bat droppings.

They are far from the mouth of the cave when the terrible roars begin deep within the monkey's throat. The girl and the German crouch by the wall. In vain, they cover their ears. The sounds are unbearable. The walls tremble. Loose stones rain down as the terrible roars rush through the cave and out the monkey's mouth.

He is standing under the tree. He is calling to her. He is trying to make himself heard above the monkey's roars. He is trying to make her see him. But the girl can't see or hear him. The girl is still in the cave with the German: they are crouching in the corner while the monkey roars.

It is suddenly raining. Raining hard. The German and the old man hear the rain hitting the leaves. The leaves tremble. But the water goes no further than the leaves.

There are so many leaves they keep the rain from falling to the earth. The German looks up at the leaves. He laughs because he and the girl are dry.

But the girl doesn't know that it is raining. She hasn't moved from the corner of the cave where she crouches with the German. She hears nothing but the monkey's roars.

He can see in her eyes that she is far away. What is there is only the shell of the girl. He can see that. But he can't see that she has taken herself away to the cave in the monkey's mouth. He only sees in her eyes that she is far away.

He is still trying to find her. He is still trying to get inside her eyes. But he doesn't know how to do it. He doesn't know how to dive into the watery sea of her eyes. He has never seen eyes like hers before.

As he wonders what to do, he sees her blink. Then blink again. She is coming back. He sees her there. She is waking from the dream. At last, she sees him. She looks up, sees the monkey high in the tree, hears the rain.

They follow the old man through the jungle. The rain is still falling. The rain muffles the monkeys' roars. To the girl, the monkeys' roars sound as though God has pressed a pillow to their faces.

The sky is dark and heavy with clouds. The sky is streaked with paths made by jittery birds. But they can barely see the sky through the trees.

The German stops to look at the trees and the plants. He bends down to look at the mimosa: the leaves close at his touch. To the small boy inside the German, this is magic. The small boy has wide eyes. He is easily pleased by nature. Nature has only to be there. And the small boy is pleased.

The girl smiles at the German, smiles at the small boy inside the German. He is a likeable boy. A curious boy who stops and listens to the cry of a bird. The small boy is now part of the dream.

The rare sight of an animal the old man calls an "ants-bear" has made the German forget the girl's eyes. The eyes that couldn't see him. The eyes that were far away. He didn't think there was anything that could make him forget the girl's eyes. But the sight of the anteater trapping termites on its tongue has made him forget.

The girl is looking at the anteater too. But the anteater hasn't made her forget the cave, the loose stones, the terrible roars as she and the German crouched in the corner. The ordeal in the cave makes her feel close to the German.

They walk on. In a flat voice, the old man tells them the local names of all the living things. The German listens. He likes the way the names sound. He repeats them. The trees and plants, the animals and birds seem more alive when he knows what to call them. He stores the names in his mind. He will tell his girlfriend the names when he sees her, when he tells her what the jungle was like. When he goes home. If he ever goes home.

In the afternoon, they return to the room in the green house. The German lies on the bed looking up at the shadows. The girl falls asleep beside him. Outside, the light is growing dim. In this room full of shadows, the German can think. The shadows don't distract him from thinking.

He is thinking about the sleeping girl. He envies her because she doesn't have to work. At home, he quits his job as soon as he has enough money to go to the tropics. He wants only to go from place to place. His mother used to cry when he quit his jobs. But now she knows there is nothing she can do.

The German thinks about the girl's eyes. They are light eyes. Eyes so light they seem to have no color of their own. They seem to take on the colors that surround them. They look green in the jungle. Blue under blue sky. Sometimes they turn dark. In the jungle, they had suddenly turned dark. He was afraid of those dark eyes in the jungle. He looks over at the girl. She is still asleep. He feels better seeing her eyes closed.

He thinks about the girlfriend. The girlfriend has blue eyes. Unlike the girl's eyes, the eyes of the girlfriend are always blue. He sighs a long sigh. What is his girlfriend seeing now? he wonders. Even when they were together he wondered how the world looked through her eyes. The thought that he would never see the world through her eyes made him feel sad and alone.

There is a tightness in his chest when he sees the girlfriend in his mind. His throat feels suddenly dry. The thought that he tried to hold back is coming forward. He can no longer stop the thought: what if somebody else is touching his girlfriend?

He glances at the sleeping girl. For a moment he wishes that he were alone. When he was alone, he didn't doubt his girlfriend. He was sure that she was true. Since he touched the girl he is afraid that somebody else is touching his girlfriend. Now he needs the girl because he is afraid.

He doesn't want to be alone anymore. At first, he liked to be alone. He liked waking up in strange towns. He liked walking the streets and meeting strangers. He liked sharing meals, and listening to travelers' tales. He liked drinking beer with the locals even though he drank too much.

But there came a moment when he wanted to see a familiar face. He had with him the address of a German he had met in his home town, a German who lives in Costa Rica. So he went there. He stayed with him a while. He helped the man build his house.

He grew attached to the man. He would ride with him on his motorcycle. He would hold him tight around the waist. He liked the way his body felt. He was surprised by his feelings. He kept those feelings which surprised him to himself.

Maybe he was afraid of those feelings. Maybe the force of those feelings made him decide to leave. He felt like traveling, he told the man. The man would soon be traveling too. He would be meeting some friends, he said.

They had agreed to meet in Belize in one month, but only the German arrived on schedule. The man from Costa Rica arrived early. But he checked out of the guest house before the German arrived. The German didn't know why he had left or where he had gone. It was then that he met the girl.

The German looks at the sleeping girl. He is glad she is there. Even though her eyes are strange. Everyone is strange, he decides. That's how people are. He doesn't want to think about her eyes anymore.

He starts to touch her. She is soft and damp. It comforts him to touch her body. To know that she is there. He parts her legs. Half-asleep, she opens herself to him. She lets him go deep inside her.

As they move together, her eyes still closed, she sees a herd of animals far away on a plain. In her dream, she thinks of them as horse tigers, the Roman name for zebras someone told her once. Their hooves kick up the dust. They move so fast they are nothing but beautiful blurs. She and the German move fast like the animals. His long hair brushes her face like the tails of horse tigers. The creatures rush toward her. There is only the sound of their hooves, and the dust, as she and the German cry out.

Later, when the sky is dark, they look up at the stars. The stars hang there in the sky like out-of-focus jewels. A veil of mist keeps them vague. The girl and the German cross the field. They follow the dirt road away from the river, to a bar at the other end of the village.

Brand new electric lamps make yellow pools of light on the road. In the distance, the yellow pools of light look like beads in a necklace to the girl. She and the German haven't walked very far when the fields come to an end. The road is surrounded by jungle. In the jungle, cicadas make sawing sounds. But the girl and the German hear more than cicadas. They hear the sound of death.

Big black beetles crash into the electric lamps. The stunned beetles hang in the air for a moment before the life in them gives out. The beetles fall like rain. A heavy black rain. A rain of death. Little mountains of death surround the lampposts which rise like strange plants. While the beetles kill themselves, the lamps shine on their glistening shells.

How strange everything looks, everything feels to the girl. The strangeness finds its way inside her, makes her strange to herself. The blackness of the jungle is all around them, is inside her. She looks up at the stars. The stars try to shine but the yellow lights won't let them.

If only she could dream the dirt road, the yellow lights, the beetles crashing. If she could dream, she wouldn't feel strange anymore. In the dream, this road, these lights, these crashing beetles would belong to her. But when she closes her eyes, the beetles are not there. The things she sees in the world cannot belong to her until she dreams them.

She holds the German's hand tighter. She needs him here. She needs him to come between her and the strangeness. She sees him in the midst of this strangeness: she sees him as the one who holds her hand, who keeps her from disappearing into the strangeness. There is his hand, only his hand stopping her, saving her.

The girl and the German are walking past the lamps and the little mountains of death. They walk a long way. Their shoes are smeared with beetles. They wonder if they missed the bar when they see a bluish light between the trees. The girl sighs with relief.

There is a low building with a thatched roof. An open door. A bench outside. A tall man sits on the bench with a beer. He is lighting a cigarette. There is a short man standing. "Hello," they say to the girl and the German.

The girl and the German go inside. The room is low. There are small wood tables and stools. A bulb hangs on a wire. The mudbrick walls were once a color. But it's impossible to tell which one. The floor is packed earth.

She can dream in this bar at the end of the world. The

mudbrick walls don't stop her from dreaming. In her dream, she can pass through the walls and drop off the edge of the earth. For a little while, she floats in the blackness. The world grows small. It spins away. She comes back when a man serves them beer.

She looks out at the night. She shudders despite the heat. She wouldn't want to be alone here. How long will she and the German be together? she wonders. But she doesn't want to think about that. She wants only to be here within the mudbrick walls. The walls make her feel safe. The walls enclose her like the German's arms in the bed in the green house.

She looks over at the German. He is someone she has always known, she is thinking. It took her some time to see him. She didn't realize when they met that he was the one she had always known. She forgets that she had always known the others too, the ones before the German.

She closes her eyes to see the German more clearly. In her dream, he is tall, his eyes are blue-green like the sea. But she is not disappointed when she opens her eyes and looks at him. It doesn't matter that he is shorter, that his eyes are bluer than the sea. He is still the one she has always known.

She closes her eyes again. She sees his body. His beautiful body above hers. His beautiful body moving. The muscles in the arms clearly defined. He is inside her. Moving in, moving out.

She feels a wave of desire. She rides the wave. Then feels it dissolve in the heat of the room. The room is hot and buzzing with insects. But the beer is cold. She takes a sip.

The short man who was outside sits down with the girl and the German. A man of mixed blood. He is drunk. He sways on the stool. His straw hat hides his eyes. They see only the mustache and the mouth which is loose like a door swinging open. He leans forward. He's been fired from his job, he says. He was the secretary of something something. They can't understand his words even though he speaks English. His words are slurred.

The German doesn't want to hear his words. He doesn't want to see this man with spittle coming from his mouth. The German turns his head, disgusted. The man whines. Tears fall down his cheeks. Tears fall on the table.

The German is angry because the drunk is sloppy. He lets his emotions fly all over. He dumps his emotions on whoever is there. The German isn't there to listen to the drunk. "You better pull yourself together!" he says.

The girl has no feeling about the drunk. She hears the sounds coming from his mouth. But she doesn't try to make sense of them. She doesn't try to understand. The drunk is just a drunk to the girl. He could be a picture of a drunk. He could be made of cardboard or plastic. He is just something that is there. She no longer hears the drunk even though he goes on and on. She no longer sees him. She has dropped off the edge of the world again. She is floating in the blackness. But the German brings her back when he takes her hand to leave.

3

It's early in the morning. The sky is not yet a color. God has just begun to stain the sky blue. The blue is pale at first as it spreads across the sky. When the sun is higher, the blue will harden. The sky's blue roof will look hard enough to crack the skulls of birds. But at this hour, there is only a hint of blue.

The fast, dark river curls through the jungle. Kingfishers flit from tree to tree along the banks. Great blue herons and white egrets sail over the murky water. A hawk makes circles in the air. The melancholy cooing call of a trogon comes from deep within the trees. The high whistle of a tinamou sounds nearby.

The canoe moves slowly upriver. The girl and the German are going to see more monkeys. The old woman's nephew guides them. They are glad to be out on the river. The room feels so small. The village feels so small. Even the jungle feels small.

The nephew points out tall cohune palms along the banks. The fronds look like giant feathers. Heavy nuts hang down in clusters. He says the fronds are used to make thatch. The nuts are used to make cooking oil and soap.

The girl and the German have seen many cohune palms. Didn't the old man point them out yesterday? Didn't he say the same things the nephew is saying? Maybe it was the day before yesterday or the day before that. They no longer remember how many days and nights they have been here.

They won't admit it but they are growing tired of the village and the jungle. At night they cool off in the little bars near the river. The lie in bed most of the afternoon. Sometimes the room is so hot they do nothing but lie there. They close their eyes. Soon the German is asleep. But sometimes the girl stays awake even after the big midday meal. She hears the German's even breathing. She opens her eyes. She lies there looking at him. He is naked. But she doesn't touch him. The heat of the day keeps her from touching him.

She is aware of the heat, but she is barely aware of the jungle now. She no longer sees the plants, the trees, the insects, the birds, the animals the way she saw them in the dream. She no longer smells the damp jungle. She barely hears the roars of monkeys, the cries of birds. She sees only his arms, his shoulders, his chest, his thighs. She smells only the scent of his hair, his body. She feels only the smoothness of his skin. She hears only his voice. The blue she sees is not the sky: it is the color of his eyes.

The German has become a place. He is the place where she is. She has crawled inside this place that is him. He is all around her the way the jungle was all around her. She feels the blood pulsing through his body. She feels his heart beating. He is too real the way the jungle was too real. She wants to run away from this place that is him. She wants to, and she doesn't want to.

When the sun is lower, they take pails of rain water down to the shower stall. The German dips the metal coffee can into the pail and pours water over the girl. Then he soaps her body. She stands there, lets him wash her. She looks up at the sky as though the sky didn't exist a moment ago. The sky is there just for them. She feels like embracing the sky. She feels like kissing it. It's a fleeting feeling. But every time he bathes her, she feels this way.

Every day from the upstairs porch, the old woman and her grandchildren look out into the field and watch the girl and the German bathe. Sometimes the old man is there too. Their white bodies make him spit in disgust.

Sometimes when they are bathing, the girl and the German do it in the shower stall. But most of the time they do it in the room. Sometimes, they do it in the morning, late in the afternoon, and again in the night. They have nothing else to do but walk in the jungle or go out on the river. Whatever they do, the heat keeps them from going very far.

On the trails, they copy the old man: they break off branches to beat mosquitoes off their backs. The heat and the bugs sap their energy, their enthusiasm. The jungle is only a place now to beat mosquitoes and wipe the sweat off their bodies.

The girl is sitting between the German and the nephew in the canoe. While the two men paddle upstream, the girl is looking at the German's back. She can't take her eyes off his back. She wants to reach out and touch him. But he is too far away to touch with her hands, with her body. So she is touching him with her eyes. Her eyes swim in the expanse of smooth skin.

The German stares at the water as he paddles. Sometimes he sees the water, sometimes he doesn't: his eyes look glazed. Thoughts come and go. They flow through him. They no longer belong to him. Sometimes he looks at the thoughts as though someone else is thinking them. If only someone else could think his thoughts, and leave him in peace.

If he were touching the girl now, he would only be aware of touching her. He would only be aware of pleasure. If only he could immerse himself in the pleasure of her body. If he could stay there in her body, he would feel no pain.

In the canoe on the river, he stares at the water so he doesn't see the thought he has tried so hard to submerge. Despite his efforts, the thought is breaking through to the surface again. Suddenly he sees the thought not only in the water, but in the trees, in the vines, in the leaves, in the air: what if somebody else is touching his girlfriend?

The thought brings on the pain. The thought makes him want to touch the girl more. Touching the girl will take away the thought, take away the pain, the uncertainty. Touching the girl is a drug.

He is staring at the water. But staring at the water isn't enough. He sees in his thoughts the girlfriend slipping away. Before his eyes, she is slipping away like water.

Before he touched the girl, he wrote to the girlfriend every few days. He had nothing to hide. But now he can't write. He stares at the water, but he sees the girlfriend. She is small, far away, vague.

The girl is looking at his back as though his back is a place where she can stay forever. She is looking at his back as though the power of wanting can bring what she wants to pass.

He feels her eyes, turns around. He asks if she's all right. He feels guilty thinking about the girlfriend while he feels her eyes on him.

When she isn't touching the German with her eyes, with her hands, with her body, she goes into her dreams so she doesn't feel alone. In her dreams, he is touching her.

In the room when he was touching her, the dream was only a veil of clouds. The clouds dissolved when he entered her body. Sometimes, she disappeared in the blueness of his eyes. But when she came back, she was afraid. She was afraid that next time she would never come back.

As he paddles on the river, she looks at his body. She knows this body. She has touched this body. Every part of this body. She wants to touch this body more. When the wanting gets too painful, she goes into the dream.

In her dream, she sees his hands on her breasts, his face lost between her legs. She breathes fast. She replays the moments of pleasure. But the pleasure he gives her is more than a dream. The dream can't give her that pleasure.

While the monkeys roar in the distance, the nephew, a musician in a band down south in Stann Creek, tells the German about the music that he plays. A special music with an African rhythm. Talking about the music makes the German forget about the girlfriend and the girl.

The girl tries to stop dreaming. She tries to stop wanting him. She listens to them talk about the music in Stann Creek. She tries to hear nothing but their words. When that doesn't work, she looks at the trees: the giant guanacastes, the strangler figs, the mampolas.

She is practicing. She is looking out at the trees as though she is all eyes. Nothing but eyes. The trees are trunks and branches and leaves, with vines winding round them. Some of the trees are in front, some in back. There are shadows. Many shades of green. The leaves have different shapes. Each tree has a different way of holding its branches. A different way of meeting the world. That's what she sees. While she sees them, the German isn't there. For a little while she has done away with the German, who is still talking to the nephew about the music, as they paddle upstream in the canoe.

The monkeys start roaring louder than ever before. Suddenly, they are all around them in the trees. The German stops talking about the music. His face changes. The small boy comes to life. The terrible sounds take over the river. There's no space for the things that grow. The sound traps the trees, the water, the air. Nothing moves until the sounds stop.

When the sounds stop, there's a space in the world where the sound has been. There's an emptiness. As though the air has been sucked out. The girl sees the emptiness, feels the emptiness. The emptiness is green and studded with sharp spines and prickly bamboo and the huge boils of termite nests in the forks of trees. The emptiness is brown and gurgling. She sees it in the whirlpools and the changing currents of the river. She sees it in the sky which goes up, up, forever up. She looks to the German to fill it. But the German, filled with wonder, is still the small boy.

He too sees the space in the world where the sound has been. But the space fills him with wonder. They wait there in the canoe for the world to fill the space. Finally, the birds come back. The swallows. The vultures. The blackbirds. Insects buzz again. A crocodile slides into the river from the bank.

When the space left by the sound is filled, the small boy is replaced by the German. Something is not quite right to the German even though the birds and the insects are back. The girl's eyes are strange again, strange in a way that he hasn't seen before. He didn't want to think about the girl's eyes even though sometimes when she looks at him, he has the feeling she is seeing someone else. Now even with his back to the girl, he feels the pull of her eyes. Even when she looks up at the sky, he feels those eyes wanting more than anyone can give.

He jumps into the river. The girl laughs. "You're brave!" she says. She wouldn't jump into this river. This river has whirlpools, hidden currents, crocodiles.

He feels the shock of the water. Maybe the shock of the water will make him forget the girl's eyes. The water is surprisingly soft like the girl. There is more to the girl than the eyes which made him jump into the water. There is this softness which draws him to her.

He thinks about this softness when he climbs back into the boat. But he doesn't think about it for long. They change direction, head downstream. He forgets about the girl while he and the nephew talk about the bands in Stann Creek.

While she listens, she wants to take his hands, and place them on her body. Right now. While he is talking. But she doesn't do that. She dangles her fingers in the water. She stares at her fingers, at the water, without seeing.

The children wait for the girl and the German on the bank. The beauty claps her hands when she sees the canoe. Like little animals they circle the pair as they walk up the path from the water. They flutter round them, stepping on their toes.

She looks into the face of the beauty. The smiling dimpled beauty. The beauty is missing four front teeth. The girl and the beauty are in love with each other. The beauty takes her hand, looks into her eyes and laughs while her sister takes the hand of the German.

The German surprises the girl. He bends over so the sister can climb on his back. Her hands clasp his neck. Her legs wind around him. He carries her up the road. The sister laughs. The beauty laughs too as she watches the German carry her sister. The girl is smiling. She likes the way the German laughs with the sister.

The beauty is pulling the girl. She is excited. She wants to show her something. She pulls her off the road into the field. She is running now between the cows, the bulls, dragging the girl behind her. There, on the fence. There it is. The skin of a snake. A big snake. The snake skin is drying on the fence. It's a tommygoff, the beauty tells her. A deadly snake. The girl looks at the snake. She knows it as a fer-de-lance. The German, still carrying the sister, comes to look too.

They all look at the snake. They are like a strange family. That's what passes through the girl's mind. This is a strange loving family. The sister is in love with the German the way the beauty is in love with the girl. The sister pulls at his long hair as he carries her.

The German has seen another snake. This one is lying on the road. They walk back. There it is, hit by a cinderblock, then run over by a truck. A coral snake. Also poisonous. This is a place of snakes, this village. The girl and the beauty bend over, look at it closely. It is covered with dust from the road. The beauty cleans the dust off its flattened body with her hand. The head is shattered.

The German can't bend down with the sister on his back. But he looks. While he looks, the beauty and her sister are shouting in Creole. The girl and the German hear the excitement in their voices. They don't feel the need to understand their words.

As they walk toward the house, they stop by one of the bars to buy the children soft drinks. They sit outside on a bench with the little girls. The owner of the bar sits inside. It's cooler there in the dark. He talks about his wife who passed away. "She's gone five weeks and two days," he tells the girl.

His wife of forty-two years. He is a mulatto. He has white hair. The girl finds him handsome even though he has very few teeth.

She and the German wave to another old man in the bar and grocery across the road. Before they go on, they stop and say hello. All day he sits in a chair by the door, propped up with pillows. He looks out at the road. He can't work anymore, he told the girl. Before he had the stroke, he planted two hundred trees. Every seed he planted grew. But now he can only wait to die. "The doctor told me not to drink Pepsi, so instead," he laughs, "I drink Coke."

They turn off the road, and stop at the vat filled with rain water behind the police station. The German fills two large pails for their next bath. The girl carries one pail. The German carries the other. The sister—no longer on his back—skips alongside him, holding his hand.

The girl has forgotten the German now. She is loving the beauty and the beauty is loving her. They are walking to the house, drunk with love. Across the field, the old woman is shouting at the beauty and her sister. "Come over here right now!" But they pay no attenion.

The beauty and her sister stay close to the girl and the German. They hold their hands for as long as they can. The beauty and her sister know something the girl and the German don't know. They know the girl and the German will be leaving very soon. The children see their leaving in the air. It is floating there, as real as the cows and the trees, the sky and the water.

Part Three

1

They are standing by the house in the middle of the night, looking at the stars. The night is passing. Soon the night will be gone. They are standing on the edge of a moment. They are coming to the end of what they know.

Something different is about to happen. The sky is about to change. A breeze is about to blow. There is a need in them for a different sky, for different trees and plants and rivers.

The way they find themselves outside on the road before dawn, waiting for the only bus of the day is inevitable. They didn't need to discuss it. They both knew it was time to leave.

They are sitting on their duffels, half-asleep. The air is thick. So thick it is hard to breathe. The world is blue-gray at this hour. The stars are gone. There is no clear division between earth and sky. The houses have soft edges. The jungle is blurred. The road is barely there.

The bus is coming. It's getting louder. They see a vague form pushing through the blue-gray air. The bus stops. They are suddenly on the bus. It's a mystery how they got there. A moment ago they were on the side of the road. They have no memory of climbing the steps, taking their seats. But there they are. They let the bus move them. They lie back and close their eyes.

After a while the bus stops. Set back from the road, the girl and the German make out a large boxlike building with many windows. There are no trees anywhere. It's as though there were never any trees. But along the road, whenever they opened their eyes and looked out the windows, the girl and the German saw nothing but trees.

Now, in the blue-grayness, they see nothing but the boxlike building and the long line of Creoles walking from the bus to the factory. The land is so empty the Creoles seem to be walking on air.

The Creoles going to work enter the girl's dreams. She sees them with her eyes closed, walking in the blue-gray air, as the bus carries her far away from the factory. Most of the Creoles have opened the factory door, and gone inside. But there are stragglers still walking as the girl continues to dream of them.

Dreams come and go as the girl and the German move in and out of sleep. While the bus carries them toward the city, they dream of skies they've never seen before; they dream of trees and rivers, animals and people, but their dreams are not the same.

A plan is forming in the German's mind while he drifts in and out of sleep. He sees the road going west through Belize. He sees a large town near the Guatemalan border. He'll stay over in that town. Maybe he'll stay a few days. Then he'll cross the border. He'll go and see the ruins and volcanoes, the mountains and the villages. He had planned to see that country before he met the girl.

The girl isn't part of his plan. Still, he sees her with his eyes closed. She stays there in his mind. He feels her body next to him. Her warm body. To get away from her, he takes a very deep breath, he goes very far inside himself. He is alone now. Alone in western Belize. Alone in Guatemala.

But he comes back. He is like a diver who was holding his breath too long. He can't stay so far inside himself. He comes back to her. Her warm body. Her warm body stands between him and his plan. Her warm body weighs on him like a stone. As he goes in and out of sleep, he is sinking in strange waters with the weight of her.

The girl sees a blackness before her eyes. In that blackness, she can just make out a jungle. She is alone in that jungle. She doesn't want to be alone. She looks for him. But she can't find him even though she feels his body next to hers.

Her eyes open. She looks at him sleeping. He is not in her jungle. His lips are apart. She listens to his breathing. Where is he? she wonders.

The girl, as though walking around in his mind, knows that he will leave her. A few times he talked about western Belize and Guatemala. The girl listened. She saw the look in his eyes. She saved his words so that his leaving wouldn't surprise her.

A dream takes shape in her mind while she thinks about his leaving. The jungle in her dream is a jungle down south. A jungle she has never seen. A jungle where jaguars roam in the night. She wants to see this jungle. She wants to embrace this jungle the way she embraced the German.

He is far away. She sees that as he sleeps. He has left her. He has continued his journey. It won't be so bad without him. She will be in the jungle again, close to the birds, the animals, the trees. She listens to her voice say these words as she drifts in and out of sleep. She wonders if this voice belongs to her.

He is quiet when the bus drops them off outside the station in Belize City. He leaves her for a moment to ask what time the next bus is going west. He is working up the courage to tell her. The man in the station says a bus is leaving in a few minutes. He wants to catch that bus. When he comes back to the girl, he holds his breath. Then he tells her. He's looking down at the ground. He waits. She doesn't say anything. He gives her a sidelong look.

Then he looks right into her face. But he can't see her. She is hiding behind her eyes. The voice comes from a girl who is far away. She is going south, she says. He sees then that her body is wooden. He is suddenly sorry. So sorry. He would take her with him if only she would come out of hiding. But she's not coming out. She's staying in there. She's found a niche inside herself. A place where she can hole up for as long as she wants.

They are standing on the street outside the bus station. The street is noisy. There are cars and taxis. Motor cycles. Horns honking. The air is thick with smoke. Men stand around. Taxi drivers look for fares. Groups of small boys yell. The street is like a fake street to the girl. The sky is fake too. A big piece of blue cardboard is in the place where the sky should be.

He takes her in his arms. He kisses her. He keeps on kissing her even though the men on the street make remarks. The taxi drivers are laughing.

She is far away even though he holds her in his arms. He can't find her in the body that he holds. Her face is turned toward the cardboard sky. He has stopped kissing her. But he doesn't want to let her go. He doesn't want to see it end like this. He's not sure he wants to see it end at all.

Still he pulls himself away. Only when her arms are by her side does he realize how tightly they held him. Those wooden arms. He thinks of those wooden arms as he rushes toward the bus. He boards it, breathless. The bus is already moving as he takes a seat. The girl is out of sight, gone.

The bus passes through the city. The German looks out the window at the clapboard houses, the dirty yards, the clothes on the lines. He's not sure what he feels. There's relief. But also there's pain.

As the bus rolls along the open road, he sees her face. Why didn't he tell her to come with him? He asks himself this. But he knows why. It wasn't just the thought of the girlfriend that stopped him. The girl scares him. Those eyes. But it's not just those eyes. His feelings for her scare him too. His feelings weighed him down. He couldn't breathe. He wants to breathe, to spread his arms, to be light as air.

A radio on the bus is playing latin songs. He listens to the words, the melodies. The songs bring him back to the moment. He feels light listening to the songs. He looks with interest and curiosity at the people in the bus: Mayans, mestizos, Creoles. He feels happy to be sitting among them.

He leans back, looks out the window, follows the flat green fields, the blue sky with little white clouds. He lets the girl fade in his mind. He lets the farm house, the jungle, the monkeys fade. While he is moving it is easy to let go of what has passed. Later, the girl, the room, the jungle, the monkeys will come back. But at this moment, he is full of the flat green fields, full of the sky.

Miles slip by, one after another. When the German thinks about the girl, he sees what passed between them as a story. As a story, it is no longer painful. It's just a story with a beginning, a middle, and an end.

He sees her body. Not the wooden body on the street. But the soft warm body. He sees the breasts. The thighs. Sometimes, when he looks out the window, he sees their bodies moving together in place of the road, the fields, the cars.

While he is looking out the window in the bus, the girl, who isn't ready to go south, heads back to the guest house in the city.

But the guest house doesn't look the same. The guest house is a shell. A dirty white shell. The rooms are full of emptiness. The girl would like to open all the doors, let the emptiness out. But instead, she locks herself up inside the room with the emptiness. She wraps it around her, feels it penetrate every pore.

A little later, she goes out, finds a cafe by the river, sits there for hours, feeling his absence. His absence is a presence so strong she can touch it, taste it, smell it. She is filled with his absence. She is full enough to burst. But she doesn't burst. She sits there looking at the river as it empties into the sea.

Later, she goes back to the guest house, walks upstairs. She is thinking she will always feel his absence. But there is a moment when she forgets. It is the moment when she hears the word, "Hello." She had forgotten this word. She looks at the man who said it. He is sitting at the table in the common room. He is a white man. But he is dark like a Carib Indian. She's never seen white skin turned so dark by the sun.

She wonders at his accent. "British?" "No, Australian," he says. She keeps looking at the darkness of his skin. She sits down. He is handsome except for his eyes. Looking in them, she sees only her reflection. She swims in his empty eyes.

His motor bike is downstairs. A terrible big macho bike. She saw it when she came in. He was going south, he says, until heavy rains washed out the road. The girl opens her eyes wide. "There's no road going south?" she says. The Australian shakes his head no.

"Where are you going?" the Australian asks the girl. "West," she says. She is going west. The emptiness has vanished. She is light. She is flying. She has an excuse to join the German now. There are few main roads in Belize so he will understand, he will believe her when she tells him there was no place else to go but west. Over and over in her mind, she is saying the words: There was no place else to go but west.

2

On the bus going west, thoughts are going round and round in her mind. But she can't catch hold of them. As soon as she tries to catch hold of them, they disappear. Then they start all over again.

The thoughts try to deal with the fear. There is a lot of fear. She is sitting there with the fear. The fear won't go away. It's the fear that makes the thoughts go round and round in her mind.

She is afraid he won't be happy to see her. But she has other fears too: maybe she won't be able to find him: maybe he will be gone by the time she arrives.

If he isn't there, she will dream him. If he is, she will dream him too. But if he is sorry that she followed him, the pain will be too great for her to dream.

Once in a while her thoughts stop and she looks at the Mayan woman sitting next to her. Seeing her profile, tracing her profile with her eyes, lets her know she is here on a bus going west. She looks out the window. Maybe he saw all this, she is thinking. Maybe he touched these hills, these farms, with his eyes.

There are rolling hills near the town. There are houses on the hills. There is a river. Then suddenly they are driving down a broad street, with signs for cola and beer and hotels. She feels a closeness to the town when she sees in her mind the German walking down this crumbling street.

Men hang out near the bus stop, watch the people getting on and off the bus. They stand in the doorways of the two Chinese restaurants, and by the movie theater which is boarded up. The girl walks past them, she looks up at the houses on the high green hills. The houses are dirty white, or faded shades of pink and blue.

At a gas station, the girl asks directions to a hotel the Australian had mentioned. She is told it is two blocks away. She walks up a hill. The hotel is over a meat market. The girl laughs when she sees the sign: "Aurelio's Hotel & Meat Market." If she were here with the German, they would laugh about this sign. She would like to laugh with somebody. She would like to talk to somebody.

This is what she is thinking as she walks up the stairs and opens the door. Inside, she sees a tall man with an air of authority. He must be the owner. He is sitting at a table talking with the German, who has his back to the door. She sees him and holds her breath.

When the tall man says hello to the girl, the German turns around. At the moment when their eyes meet, the girl breathes easier. He is happy to see her. In fact, he is so happy to see her she feels as though she is dreaming. Her fear is forgotten. It's as though there was never any fear. It's as though she knew all the time that he would be happy to see her.

She can hardly breathe he is holding her so tight. He missed her, he is saying. He almost called her on the phone last night. He wanted to say that he missed her. But he didn't call. He went to a bar instead. He had one beer, then another, and another, and another. There came a point when he didn't miss her at all. He didn't miss anything. He staggered back to his room before dawn.

She didn't expect to hear him say that he missed her. She is surprised. She is happy. For a second, she is silent. Then before she is able to stop herself, she hears words coming out of her mouth, the same words she has said over and over in her mind as she prepared herself for this moment.

This moment is not turning out the way she planned. This moment is better. But she doesn't know how to change the script.

"The rains washed out the road down south," she says. "I wouldn't have come, but there was nowhere else to go." She listens to her words. She no longer knows why she is saying them.

The German looks disappointed, but he picks up her duffel and tells the tall man that she will be staying in his room.

She is only going up the stairs but she is flying. While he holds her hand and carries her duffel, she is flying. She is so happy she has forgotten about her words. He unlocks the door to the room. They go inside. The wooden blinds are shut. The room is dark. A fan blows.

The girl, who is so happy, is losing her happiness as she steps inside the room. She can feel it falling away. He wants her. She should be happy. But something has changed. She tries to see the German in her dream. But all she can see is the German who left her.

She can't see that she has changed. The fear has changed her. The fear that he will leave again stands in the place of her happiness.

He holds her in his arms, they kiss, lie down on the bed. In the dark, they try to find each other. They try to continue where they left off. His hands move over her body. But they don't feel like his hands. They don't feel like the hands of the German who made her happy.

He enters her body. But her body is without life. She

is holding back the life so he can't take it and go away. "What's wrong?" he whispers. But she says nothing. She lies there seeing a parade before her eyes of all the males who ever left her, starting with the first one who left her mother and her when she was only twelve.

In the silence, while she lies there, the German feels the loss of her. When he left her in the east, he didn't feel the loss of her as deeply as he feels it now.

As he feels the loss of her, he feels something shift inside him. Even as he feels the pain, the loss, he feels lighter, as though a weight is gone. He feels free. Suddenly he can move around inside himself. She is no longer taking up his space. She is no longer there on his mind like a stone he can't move.

She lies beneath him. She is very still. But that doesn't stop him from moaning. That doesn't stop him from coming inside her.

Afterwards, he turns on the light. He looks at her. A little while ago he felt so free. He remembers feeling free. But now he feels the loss of her again. He feels the pain. He tries to find the life in the girl. He looks for the life in her eyes. But her eyes see only the German who left her.

They dress, go out in the street. They walk around. They seem lost in thought. Then the German remembers the Mayan ruins above the town. He asks her if she wants to go and see them. Yes, she says.

They walk up a steep hill. They pass the streets, the houses, the shacks with ragged fences. The hill grows steeper. It is covered with jungle now. A winding dirt path disappears between the trees.

Seeing the jungle excites the girl. She had forgotten her dream of the jungle. She had forgotten the ferns, the orchids, the sharp spines of give-and-take palms, the peeling red bark of gumbolimbo trees. She had forgotten she is alive like all the other living things.

They are listening to the birds and insects when they see the gray stones of a temple rising between the trees.

They walk across a clearing that was once a plaza, they climb the steps of a temple. The girl feels sympathy for these stones, abandoned by the Maya. She runs her fingers over their roughness to feel their life. She feels their life flowing through her fingers, through her body.

They stand at the top of the highest temple. No one else is there at the site. The quiet presses down on them. The quiet is there between the cries of birds and the buzz of insects. The quiet is alive with Maya spirits.

They stand there looking at smaller temples and tombs and plazas below, some covered with trees. The girl talks about the quiet. She needs to talk, to put something of her own in the air.

The air is alive. The girl is alive like the air and the stones and the jungle. She feels the life inside and outside her body as her own. The quiet belongs to her too. This quiet, full of unheard sound, holds her fears, her thoughts, her dreams.

The German climbs down from the temple. He crosses a clearing, climbs up to the platform of a smaller temple. He is the small boy again, full of wonder, walking through archways in the ruined walls.

The girl climbs down, stands in the clearing, watching him. She sees him better from a distance. From a distance, he can be whomever she wants. From a distance, he can be her dream.

The girl climbs up to the platform where the German is standing. His back is turned to her. He is still the small boy looking at the stones when she comes up behind him. She throws her arms around his waist, and presses herself against his body. But the small boy breaks loose, climbs over the stones like a goat.

He's disappeared inside another temple a distance away. He's left her standing alone on the platform. But still the girl is smiling. She has found her dream. He is no longer the German who left her. In her dream, they lie naked on the stones.

When he comes back to the platform where the girl is dreaming, the sun is lower in the sky. He looks at the girl. He sees the life in her. But this time he wants to keep his distance.

He wants only to be the small boy. He wants only to feel

this lightness, this freedom. The girl follows him down to the clearing and into the jungle. He says he is taking a short-cut through the jungle to the top of the hill nearby.

The jungle is thick and tangled. The tangled roots and vines make the girl forget her dreams. From the ruins, she had seen a path to this hill through the trees. "Why don't we take the path?" she calls out. But the German doesn't answer. He is the small boy. The small boy is having fun. He is climbing over rotted trees. He is wading through the mud.

The girl is angry. She is tripping over roots and vines. But the roots and vines are not the reason for her anger. She is thinking about the German. She is thinking about the way he broke loose from her arms: the way he ran off at the ruins.

She seems to forget that only a while ago when he touched her in the room, she forced herself not to feel: she forced herself to act dead in his arms. The German has not forgotten, but when he is being the small boy he feels no pain.

There is nothing to excite the small boy at the top of the hill. There is only a restaurant. The restaurant is a huge place with a thatched roof and unpainted walls.

It is late in the afternoon when the girl and the German sit down at a table overlooking the valley. They do not speak to each other.

Most of the tables are pushed to one side. A reggae band is rehearsing. When they break, the German talks to the musicians. The kitchen is closed, but a waiter serves them beer. The band plays the same songs over and over.

The sun is setting. The girl is no longer angry. She looks at the sky. The sky is a strange smokey blue. There is also a deep purple and a hint of gold. But it's the smokey blue she didn't expect to see. It's a strange color for an evening sky.

The German is sitting beside her, staring into space. He taps his fingers in time to the music. The girl looks at him. He is so distant, she is thinking.

He is trying to stay free of her. Like the small boy who stayed free of her at the ruins and in the jungle, the German in the restaurant is trying to keep his distance.

She opens her mouth to say something. But she has nothing to say. The dream isn't there. She doesn't know the German without the dream. She feels lost without the dream. What she says to him is only words.

When he talks to her, he looks at the band playing, or he looks at the purple in the sky. His words don't seem to come from him.

The sky is dark. She sees that the darkness makes him dream. He's dreaming out loud about his friend, the man he stayed with in Costa Rica. He's telling her little stories about him. His face looks softer as he dreams. His friend in Costa Rica has replaced her, she is thinking.

They leave the restaurant, walk down the dirt path. In the distance, they see the lights of the town. They hear the sawing sound of cicadas. But they also hear something else. A familiar crashing sound. They look up and see big black beetles crashing into the street lamps along the path on the hill.

Seeing the beetles makes her sad because the beetles remind her of being happy. Last time she saw them she remembers being happy. She wonders if the happiness she remembers is only a dream she is dreaming now.

The girl and the German are standing at the door of the hotel. It's an awkward moment. He's quiet. Then he says it. He's going out alone. He needs to be alone. The girl doesn't say anything. She nods her head, goes inside, sees the long night before her.

3

She stretches out on the bed, her eyes closed. Her hand pats the pillow, the sheet. He's not there. The room is dark. The wooden blinds are shut. The morning light can't touch the room.

She opens the wooden blinds, lets in the light. But she can't see it. Her darkness gets in the way. In her darkness, she looks for a ray of hope. Maybe he came back while she was sleeping. Maybe he left before she awoke.

She gets dressed. Maybe she will find him in the restaurant next door. The one owned by the Brit. He told her all the foreigners go there. She goes downstairs to the restaurant, she looks for him outside at the tables in the back.

The German is writing postcards. There is someone with him. She can only see the back of her head, the long red hair. He sees her coming. He says something to the red-haired girl. The red-haired girl rises, goes over to another table where friends of hers are sitting.

"Who is that?" asks the girl. "A student," he says. "I met her last night in a bar." He looks down at the postcards, but he doesn't see them. He feels suddenly confused. Guilty. Seeing the girl makes him feel guilty. Why should he feel guilty? He no longer feels guilty when he thinks about the girlfriend. The girlfriend seems so far away. The red-haired girl has pushed the girl-friend even farther away in his mind.

They say nothing more about the red-haired girl. But the girl sees him glance more than once in her direction. She tries to eat, but she can hardly bring a forkful of food to her mouth. She glances at the red-haired girl, then she looks away. But even when she isn't looking, all she can see is the red-haired girl.

She needs to see something that will make her forget the red-haired girl She needs to see something big and dramatic like the big Mayan temple she saw in the poster at the hotel. The temple is less than an hour away. It is one of the tallest temples in the country. She tells him this. She asks if he wants to go and see it.

He would rather write postcards. While he is writing he doesn't think about anyone. He doesn't feel guilty or confused. There is nothing but the pen and the paper, and the words streaming out. But he can't tell the girl he would rather write postcards. "We can go and see the temple," he says. He looks down at the table as he says it so she doesn't see his anger. He is angry at himself. Why can't he feel free to do whatever he likes?

They go down to the open market where the bus leaves for the ruins. They wait. People mill around, some carry baskets, and try to sell them fruit. The bus comes. The bus is old, it shakes. In the bus, they sit without touching. The girl sees the face of the red-haired girl when she looks out the window. It's a short ride. They take a ferry across the river, walk up a hill in the jungle. They cross a clearing, climb the many steps to the large Mayan temple.

They stand high above the earth. There is green jungle all around them. At the edge of the world where the jungle stops, there is air and space and blueness. The girl goes to the edge, she flies off into the blueness. If only she could stay there, sailing in the blueness.

But the voice of the German brings her back. He is admiring the frieze on the side of the temple. She looks at the frieze too, until she sees the ant. On a ledge, there is an ant carrying an insect many times its size. To the girl, there is something amazing about seeing an ant so far from the ground.

When she looks at the green jungle spread-out below, she feels as small as the ant. She has an urge to step on the ant, to crush it, as though that would prove her power. But she stops herself, she watches it instead.

When she tires of the ant, she looks at the chamber above the ledge. The German has just come out of the chamber. He is standing in front of it. As she looks at the German, a dream takes over. The German is no longer the German. He is a Maya king, his head adorned with feathers, appearing for his audience below; thousands shout at the foot of the temple. She sees them as she looks down.

They are shouting because the drugged king has just emerged from the sacred chamber. The Maya king is holding the part of himself that she has felt so often inside her. But this time it is stained with blood. The Maya king has pierced it with a knife, drawn a rope through the wound, and let the blood drip on bark paper. He set the paper on fire. In the smoke he saw a vision. Near collapse, the Maya king raises his blood-stained hand, and relays a message from his ancestors. The girl sees the German as the Maya king until she hears his voice. His voice dispels the dream. She looks again at the ledge for the ant, but the ant is gone.

When they go back to town, the German leaves her by the hotel. He has to meet someone, he says. She doesn't ask if he is meeting the red-haired girl. She doesn't say anything. She goes up to the room.

She is unlocking the door when a woman stops her in the hall. A fat woman, almost middle-aged. She has just arrived, she says. She looks nervous. "Is this town safe for a woman alone? Is this hotel safe?" she asks her. The girl doesn't know. She hasn't been here long enough to know.

The girl says, "I don't know anything. Everything has been so strange since I arrived. I have this German friend... Everything was great between us back east. But then he left me to come out here." She shrugs. "I don't know why he left me." She looks at the woman as though the woman might know, the woman might have an answer.

But the fat woman doesn't know. She doesn't say anything so the girl goes on. "I knew that he would leave me. I knew before he did. But I didn't think he'd leave me so soon." She wipes her eyes. "I shouldn't have followed him. I should have let him go. There's nothing for me here, no point in my staying."

The fat woman thinks the girl is a little bit crazy. But she sees the girl's pain. She knows about pain. When the girl talks about the German, she is reminded of her husband. The fat woman had a husband once. She had been thin before he found another woman.

"He met this red-haired girl..." the girl goes on. When the girl says this, the fat woman feels an old wound split open. She feels a stabbing pain. Then she feels anger. "He should be the one to leave this town," she says. "Not you!"

The girl feels better talking to the fat woman. They make plans for tomorrow to see a waterfall together and a cave. The tall man who owns the hotel arranges day trips for his guests.

She has dinner with the fat woman. When she comes

back to the room, the German is taking a shower. He's going out again, he says. She stands there very still, hating him. She watches him shave: she watches him dress: perhaps watching him will change the course of his actions: maybe if she watches him hard enough, long enough, he'll change his mind and stay with her instead.

She stands there wishing she could hate him more. But wanting him gets in the way of hating him. She can't stop herself from wanting him.

He acts as though she isn't there. What he sees and feels now is not the girl. What he sees and feels is her wanting. All of her is there in her wanting. But she wants more than he can give.

He would like to be the kind of man who feels nothing. If he were that kind of man, he wouldn't feel confused now, he wouldn't feel afraid, he wouldn't feel sorry. But he is not that kind of man. He is the kind of man who doesn't know how to say what he feels.

How can he tell her he feels free in the arms of the red-haired girl? The red-haired girl makes no demands. She is just a girl he will forget. Even his girlfriend might understand this infatuation with the red-haired girl.

The girl slams the door, she goes over to the fat woman's room. She stays there until she hears the German leave. Then she comes back. She lies in bed. She dreams of hurting him.

He bangs on the wooden blinds late at night, he wakes her. He lost his key, he says. She lets him in. He is drunk. At first she wants to scream at him, she wants to say something hurtful. But then she sees the German in her dream.

He pulls her to him, pushes her down on the bed. He is saying things to her in German. She doesn't know if he is saying words of love or hate. He is mumbling. Even if she knew his language she might not understand.

Even while she is dreaming him, even while he is touching her, there is another dream. In that other dream, she sees the German and the red-haired girl. She sees his hands, his mouth, the hard thing pressing into her touch the body of the re-dhaired girl. She sees this, but still she lets him touch her. She is waiting for the moment when his touch will make her forget. Soon she will forget this dream with the red-haired girl. She opens herself to him so that she may forget.

He is rough when she opens herself to him. She doesn't know he is trying to rid himself of her by being rough. As though with his roughness, he can tear her from himself. His roughness makes her dream of the burlap sacks that chafed her skin in the market. She sees the men bowed down under the heavy burlap sacks. There they are in the crowded market. So many people! She is alone. Afraid. She sees snot running from the children's noses. She sees a woman suckling a baby. Her breasts look like rotting fruit. She sees a man raise his arms to fix the tarpaulin over his stall. She sees the long scar across his belly, the long dark scar. She is jammed between the men weighed down by the heavy burlap sacks. They are closing in, about to crush her when she hears herself cry out.

She opens her eyes. She is suddenly aware of being alone. The German lies there, still as death. He's asleep. She rolls out from under him, moves over to the far side of the bed.

A few hours later, he wakes up sick. He looks at the time. It is early in the morning. The girl is getting ready to go on a trip to the waterfall and the cave with the fat woman. The girl didn't know the German had planned to go there too.

He gets out of bed while the girl goes downstairs to meet the fat woman. The girl and the fat woman climb into the back of the pick-up truck with the tall man's wife and some other guests. The German is the last to board the truck. His head is pounding.

While he stares at the road, he feels the girl's eyes. She is sitting across from him, looking at his body. She imagines terrible things she would like to do to his body.

The fat woman watches the girl look at the German. Then the fat woman looks at the German too. She finds the German laughable. He is posing, she thinks to herself. He is one of those handsome men who are always posing.

The tall man's son, a boy about eleven, is sitting beside the girl in the truck. The child is pointing out the birds that fly across the road and over the trees. The girl stops looking at the German to see the birds the child is pointing out as the tall man drives through the mountains. The mountains are covered with forest. The air smells of pine.

She and the child are both pointing out the birds now. There is a yellow-tailed oriole, a black vulture, a flock of parakeets, a roadside hawk. The child is excited every time he spots a bird. The girl becomes excited too. There is more in life than the German. There is the child. There are the birds and the trees.

The tall man's wife, who sits near her son, tells the girl about the Lebanese man who owns great tracks of forest. "The Lebanese man has five wives," she says. "One of his wives wouldn't give a young lumberer time off to see his first child born. This wife got very sick soon after. She never recovered," she says with a smile.

In the pine forest, the tall man stops the truck by the side of the road to see a-thousand-foot waterfall plunging down the mountain into jungle. The bottom of the waterfall is hidden in mist. The mountains rise all around them.

The German is feeling better. The air is clearing his head. He smiles at the girl. But she turns away. She looks at the road as they drive through the mountains.

After a while, the tall man stops the truck. He leads them on foot to the mouth of a cave. They go inside. Light, from another entrance in the rock, half a mile away, filters through the cavern.

The girl hears water dripping, hears the sound of a stream, hears their voices echo. Here, the tall man says, the ancient Mayans collected holy water. In the dim light, she sees the unearthly stone garden. There are milky white crystals and cream-colored columns. There are garments carved in stone like those worn by Greek statues.

She looks in wonder at pinnacles rising from the floor, at stones shaped like ocean waves jutting from the walls. Beneath her feet, she sees stone slabs as smooth and translucent as ice, while overhead thousands of long pointed icicles hang down from the roof.

When she looks at the rocks, she feels the motion of water eating away the stone. As though the process were speeded up, she sees the rocks crack; she sees the cracks open, the way they would over the course of millions of years, allowing shimmering water to flow through the spaces.

The girl feels the cave cast a spell over her as she lies down on a bed of stone that fits the contours of her body. She may never rise again. This bed of stone was made for her body. She has found a bed of stone where she can dream.

The girl, milky and smooth, lies there as still as the stone. She is dreaming herself as a cave. She is a great dark opening in a rock wall: she is a high archway going down into the depths of her. She is high and dark and deep. There is so much space inside her.

While she lies on the bed of stone, she is dancing in this space that is herself. She is doing as she pleases. She is spreading her arms like wings. She is spinning round and round until she is dizzy.

When she isn't dreaming herself as a cave, she is watching the German. She has only to tilt her head. He moves so gracefully over the stones. He is the small boy again. How light he looks. He seems to be a creature made only of air. It hurts her to look at him so she closes her eyes, and dances through the cave within her.

4

When she leaves the cave with the others, she is still in the cave of her dream. She comes out of the dream only when they reach the river. The river is making its way down from the mountains over giant boulders that are worn smooth. Deep pools have formed between the rocks. The pools of water are pale green.

The smooth stones make natural slides. The tall man's son slides down a stream of water into a pool. The fat woman follows him, making small high-pitched sounds.

The German is climbing the rocks. They are steep and slippery. The water is flowing down over them. The girl fears for the German even while she sees him in a dream gracefully falling through the air before he splatters on the rocks.

But there is a deeper dream in her than the dream of seeing him fall. There is the dream that he will want her the way he wanted her in the green house while the howler monkeys roared.

She closes her eyes. She sees him climbing the rocks. He looks over, sees her watching him. He smiles, climbs down, comes over to where she is standing, takes her hand. Together, they go back to the rocks he was climbing. Up and up they go. They are climbing to a waterfall.

The rocks by the waterfall look like fake rocks. They are as smooth and shiny as satin. He takes her hand. He leads her. Carefully, they climb behind the water. The waterfall is like a curtain. They are hidden by the water.

The water is crashing down all around them. The sound drowns out their voices. But there is nothing to say that the water isn't already saying. The water is a celebration.

No one can see them here. They take off their swim suits. Their bodies press against one another. They are the feel of wet skin, the touch of body against body. That's all there is. That and their breathing and the water crashing down.

Then there is more. There is the opening up, the fullness of him coming into her body. There is the sound of birds even though there is nothing but the sound of water and breathing. There are more and more birds; clicks, whistles, chirps, high notes, low notes, the same note over and over, even though there is nothing but the sound of water and breathing.

She opens her eyes. She sighs. She looks at him. He is not the one she has been dreaming.

He is very alone here, she is thinking. He looks like a man locked within himself. There is nothing of him showing on the surface. There is only the grace of the body. The body stopping for a second to consider its next move. She sees that the body is posing even while it climbs. It doesn't know how to forget itself. It is alone. Aware that it is alone.

The body feels less alone when it knows that others are looking at it, even though he tries to tell himself the others are nothing but eyes, admiring eyes. He tries to convince himself they are only admiring eyes.

But the body holds a memory that it was more than a pose with the girl. He is trying to push that memory out. But the memory won't go. The memory tells him that his body was alive with the girl. He was there in the body. He was the body. And the girl was there to receive his body: she opened herself to his body even though she liked to believe that his body was only her dream.

There is anger in the German at the girl. It is the anger of a man who thinks he has been seen. He is afraid that she has seen the softness in him, the softness that is there at the core of him. He is trying to erase in her the memory of his softness. He poses to hide that softness from himself and from the world.

The girl saw that softness in him, but she wanted it to be a dream. She couldn't bear to see that softness without the dream.

She wasn't apart from that softness that she saw. That softness wasn't something separate from her being. That softness was also the softness in herself, the softness still there behind her dreams.

Looking at the German now, the girl feels the softness in herself. There is no dream now that can hide the softness. She feels the softness as a wound, a deep wound, an open wound.

The girl has her swim suit on beneath her clothes. She undresses, goes into the deepest rock pool. She lets herself go down, down into the deep water. The water is warm. She lets the water dull her longing. She lets the water soothe the wound. The water frees her until her breath gives out. She comes up for air.

The longing in her is lessened not only by the water. The longing is lessened by the warmth, by the smooth round boulders, by the deep blue sky.

The others are lying on the rocks or swimming. There is longing in their bodies even though they don't know it. She can see the longing in the way the bodies show themselves to the sun, the way the bodies give themselves to the water.

Even here in the pale green water she draws strength from the dream of the cave. Her cave goes down, down, down to the depths of her. In the dream, there is space. In that space she can breathe. In that space there is life.

She is the life without form, the life that fills the space of the body, the space of the cave. The cave is the shell, the skin which protects the life, and holds it together. The cave is a boundary which makes it easy to see where she ends and the world begins.

In spite of the falling water, there is a stillness inside and outside her body. Even the people in the pools are not moving now. It's as though the world has stopped for a second. Even the butterflies and dragonflies freeze. Birds don't move from their branches.

In the stillness, the girl stays where she is; she is looking at the German who pauses on the rocks. There is something indelible in this moment. There is something she will remember in years to come. Something is stamping itself on her memory but she doesn't know what.

This moment is inside her. This stillness is the stillness underneath the movement in the world. Mostly, this stillness doesn't show itself. But here the stillness has spread itself out before her.

She allows herself to be in the stillness. The stillness is frightening. There is only this quiet life, this life without violence, without upheaval, without longing, without pain. For a second, she stands inside it. Then it is gone.

Then there is the movement of the bodies in the water again, the movement of the bodies on the rocks. The German continues his climb, the birds fly, the butterflies flutter, the dragonflies loop through the air.

As the truck drives back, the land is waving like water. The crests of the waves are the mounds of Mayan temples: buried temples sleeping under layers of earth.

The girl, riding in the back of the truck, goes up and down on the waves. There is only the motion of the truck and the sky dimming, coming down to meet the dark earth like a slow secret.

The German is sitting inside the truck with the tall man so he isn't in her vision. He isn't in her mind. She lets the sky and the waving land fill her mind.

But then the moment comes when there is only the town, the little streets, the people milling about. There is nothing big to fill her eyes, her mind.

The German says he is going to the restaurant. That's all he says. It's his way of telling her to come, but he doesn't tell her. He doesn't know how to tell her anything anymore. He doesn't know how to tell her the red-haired girl has gone.

She goes up to the room. Then she walks over to meet him at the restaurant. But when she is by the door she stops herself. She doesn't go in, she walks past it. She is trying to think, but she can't think. The words won't come.

She turns around, walks back to the door. She no longer knows what she is doing. When she turns again, she doesn't look where she is stepping. In that moment when she doesn't look, she falls into the deep gutter running along the whitewashed street.

Blood gushes from a cut on her foot, and a cut on her leg. There is blood on her sandal. The sight of the red blood against the white street, the white gutter, is horrible. She looks at it and feels the horror. She doesn't do anything for a minute or so except look at it. Then, taking the horror with her, and the pain, she goes to her room, cleans the wounds, wraps them in bandages.

The German had seen her pass by the restaurant just before she fell. He didn't know what to do. He just followed her with his eyes. He didn't know where she was going.

Now she walks into the restaurant, her leg bandaged, her foot bandaged. He has almost finished eating. He looks at her. She fell in the street, she says. She says it accusingly, as though her fall were his fault.

He laughs. It is a terrible moment. He is sorry and not sorry. He doesn't know anymore. He doesn't know anything. Suddenly, he can hardly breathe. The girl's eyes have caught him. They are animal eyes. He doesn't know this face, this anger that he sees in her eyes. He rises, says he is meeting some German travelers he met last night. He goes off, leaves her there with her anger.

The anger is still there inside her when she goes back to the room. The anger and the hurt. Where is the red-haired girl? she wonders. Who are these travelers that he met? But she doesn't want to know the answers. The answers would only bring more pain.

Only the reggae music distracts her from the anger and the pain. The music is so loud she can't even think. She goes out on the porch, sees the fat woman. Together, they stand there, listen to the music coming from a club a few streets away.

The girl has the urge to dance. She will dance the German out of her body, out of her mind. She tells this to the fat woman. "Come with me," she says. The fat woman looks at her bandaged leg and foot. But the girl has forgotten her fall.

The club is an enormous room of unplaned planks and windows without panes. The room is dark. In the pink spotlight, the local reggae band plays. A hostess guides them through the darkness to a table by the dance floor. There is no one dancing yet. But the room is filling up. Very soon the room is full.

In the darkness, the girl and the fat woman are surrounded by moving shadows, and voices that occasionally rise above the music. Strobe lights wander through the room, light up breasts, legs, more legs, more breasts. In the strobes, the girl and the fat woman glimpse long hair flying, swirling skirts, flailing arms, heads thrown back, gyrating torsos, swinging hips, jutting elbows, bodies grinding. The strobes light up the faces of the girl and the fat woman, sitting at the table by the dance floor.

Two young men are walking over to their table. One is as black as the room, the other is brown, a lightish brown. "Do you like to dance?" the very black man asks the girl. The girl says, "Yes." She follows him out on the dance floor.

The brown man asks the fat woman to dance. But the fat woman can't do it, she can't get herself to say yes. She can't get herself to stand up even in this darkness. The brown man is not bothered by her refusal. He sits down next to her. He looks small. He is still a boy really. The fat woman could be his mother.

The fat woman is uncomfortable. He is shouting in her ear, "What is your name?" She shouts back. She fingers her glass of ginger ale. Her eyes look frantically through the crowd, trying to find the girl. She doesn't feel so alone once she has found her.

The girl is dancing with the very black man who is also almost a boy. The very black man looks East Indian. He lives in the south of the country. He shouts this to her, above the music. The brown man is his brother, he says, even though the brown man looks like a mestizo.

"I am available to be your boyfriend," says the very black man to the girl when there is a short break in the music. "I am very sincere," he adds, smiling sweetly. The girl is smiling too. But she doesn't say anything. She doesn't know what to say.

She is smiling because she is happy. Dancing makes her happy. While the music is playing, she forgets about the German. She is dancing with all of herself despite her bandaged leg and foot. Her long hair is falling this way and that. She is a whirl of motion, a blur. The very black man is dancing right along with her.

The strobes stay on the girl and the very black man. The room is hot. The girl and the very black man are dripping wet, but they can't stop, don't want to stop. The same songs play over and over. They are inside the rhythm, this pounding rhythm. They are deep inside the sound. There is only this motion and this sound.

Finally, the girl and the very black man come back to the table. The fat woman looks relieved. The men buy them beer. The men smile. Sometimes they shout above the music. The girl and the fat woman try to understand their words, they shout back.

The girl is looking around the room when she sees a man who looks like the Australian she met back east. Lit by the strobe lights, she can see him dancing with two blondes. They look like models. The strobe lights stay on the Australian and the blonds.

The girl is watching them. She can't take her eyes off them. No one can dance that fast, she is thinking. It must be the strobes that make their motions look so fast. But no, it's not the strobes.

They don't look human. They are shaking, spinning, leaping. They are dancing in a frenzy. They are moving like mechanical toys wound too tight. She wonders what drug makes them dance this way.

She wonders for a little while, but then she stops wondering. She starts dreaming about the Australian. He looks handsome even while he dances in a frenzy. She is dreaming his tanned skin: the skin as dark as a Carib Indian.

She dreams that she and the Australian are dancing. The blondes are dancing too. But they dance off on their own. All night the girl is dancing with him. Then suddenly, the club is closing. It's time to leave. She hops on the back of his motor bike. They take off down the highway to the jungle in the south.

She is dreaming this when the strobes go elsewhere. She looks into the darkness, but she can't see the Australian or the blondes. She has lost the dream. In the place where the dream was, there is only this darkness, this darkness which is not a dream.

5

Late at night as she lies in bed, the girl is thinking, maybe the German will never come back. She thought the same thing last night and the night before. But some nights he comes back. He comes back while she is sleeping. He lies down, he sleeps for a little while. In a half-sleep, she feels his body close to hers. Then he takes some things to the room he rented next door.

He is getting ready to leave, getting ready to go to Guatemala. But he can't leave yet. He doesn't know how to leave the girl. So he is leaving little by little, day by day. Every day he takes a little bit more from the room.

Every day he is a little more distant except for the hours when they lie sleeping. This last closeness is hard for him to give up. But he is almost ready. Soon he will be ready, the girl knows it.

In the morning, she looks for him in the restaurant next door. "Let's walk by the river," she says. It's useless, she knows that, but still she tries. He looks at her. He is hung-over, but he can't say no, he feels too guilty.

They are leaving the town, walking in the tall grass by the river. They stop to watch the drivers hosing down their buses in the shallows. But then there is nothing to see but the shimmering river, the forest, the sky.

He is walking fast, too fast. She asks him to slow down. She wants to see where she is stepping. There could be snakes here, she is saying. But he isn't listening. He stops only when he sees the horses.

Three white horses play in the river near the opposite shore. As the horses play, the German takes off his clothes, and jumps into the river. The girl, suddenly hopeful, takes off her clothes, and jumps in after him. But they swim apart like strangers, like people who have never met.

They watch the horses shake their manes. They see the grace of their necks, their long thin legs. The horses whinny, throw back their heads, make little dance steps in the water.

The girl gets out of the water, she sits on a log watching the German. The German lifts himself onto another log, then stands there looking at the horses.

The girl looks between his legs. Before, she would have taken it into her mouth, she would have kissed it. She would have felt it grow as she licked it and kissed it.

She gets dressed, starts walking back before he has finished dressing. There is nothing left. She knows it. In his eyes, she could see that he has left for Guatemala. He has gone.

That night while she is sleeping, he writes a note saying he is sorry. He takes the last of his things. She stretches out on the bed when she awakens, but this time she knows he won't be there.

Early in the morning, she knocks on the door of the fat woman's room. She has thought of a place to go, she says to the fat woman. In the east, there is a little farming village with mango and cashew trees. Near the village are swamps with crocodiles, and lagoons where thousands of birds stop on their way back north. She will hide out there with her pain until she is ready to go some place else.

On the bus, she is looking at the two white people amidst the black and brown faces. There is a blond girl, wearing many little braids like the Creole children. She is sitting with her boyfriend. He wears a white hat. As the bus goes east, the girl stares at the blonde and her boyfriend.

When she changes buses, she tells the driver the name of the village where she wants to get off. But it's as though someone else is riding on the bus, someone she doesn't know. Maybe she is the blond girl with the many braids, riding east with her boyfriend. If only she could be the blond girl.

The bus stops. The driver calls to her. She doesn't hear. She doesn't see. It's as though the life in her is lying low, is waiting for a reason to rise to the surface.

She stares at the glass. The driver calls out again. Suddenly, she sees. There is a lagoon out the window. She steps off the bus. Here she is. Somewhere. A place. But she can't place herself.

The color is gone from the sky. She feels as though someone has taken it away just before she arrived. There are gnarled and twisted trees by the lagoon. There are birds flying.

There is no one around. She puts her duffel down on a table under a thatched roof by a house with a sign that says, "Visitors Center." It's a plain house. A wooden house. She knocks on the door. But no one is there.

A wind is blowing across the lagoon. The wind is growing stronger. The girl sits on the bench by the table, waiting for someone. Anyone. No one comes.

After a while, she walks up the road, sees a farmhouse, knocks on the door, says to the Creole woman who answers that she is looking for a room. The woman says she must wait for the man in the Visitors Center. He went home for lunch.

She goes back to the table. She waits some more. Finally, he comes. He drives her in his pick-up through the jungle to a farm house. She sees cows, chickens running around. There are clothes hanging on the lines.

A Creole woman comes outside. The girl is surprised when she sees her. Her hair is the color of wheat. She has blue eyes, fair skin. But her features are those of a black woman. She has Scottish blood, she tells the girl.

She shows her to a room. There are tiny frogs on the walls. They are very still. They almost look like decorations. There is nothing of interest in the room beside the frogs. The room is barely big enough for a bed and a chair.

The girl doesn't stay in the room. She goes out, wanders down a jungle road. By the farm houses, there are twisted trees. The trees are in pain. They suffer. She knows they suffer. She sees her pain in the trees. Their branches reach out as though there were somewhere else to go, as though if only they could reach that other place, all would be well. Even now they are reaching out, trying to get there. She too is trying to get there, to a place where the pain can't go.

She is walking down the road. There are few houses now, there is mostly jungle. There are jungle sounds, flying things. Then a long way off, standing in the middle of the road, she sees them. Four big dogs. They are very still. Then they see her and start barking. Suddenly, they are running toward her, their teeth bared. They are running fast, kicking up the dust. They are panting. She sees their mouths dripping wet, their shiny pink tongues.

They are growling, jumping up and down around her legs as she shouts at them in a voice she never heard before. A voice that is loud and sure. A voice that is a miracle. The girl is shaking. But the voice is steady. The growling dogs are backing away from the voice.

She listens to this voice that is hers, she watches the dogs back away. For a moment, the dogs come closer. But the girl shouts louder. They back away again. They are growling still, but slowly they head back the way they came. The girl, who is still shaking, heads back to the house.

The Creole woman's husband is a part-time pastor and a part-time farmer. He says this to the girl at dinner. They eat in a tiny room lit by a kerosene lantern. The walls are dirty green. There is a bright red sofa. There are little knickknacks on unpainted wooden shelves.

The husband asks about the shopping malls in America. He would like to see them some day. He asks her to tell him how they look. The girl doesn't know what to say. They don't look like anything, she tells him. There is silence. For a minute, they listen to the thunder, to the rain coming down. Lightning flashes through the room.

How can she see the lagoon? she asks them. There is a man who lives by the lagoon, they say. He can take her out in his boat. But he leaves before dawn to fish so she will have to arrange it tonight.

They call in their daughter, who is not much younger than the girl. The daughter will take her to the man who lives by the lagoon.

When they leave the house wearing rain ponchos, there is thunder and lightning, but the rain has let up. It's a long walk, a few kilometers to the lagoon. The girl follows the daughter, who carries a lantern down the jungle trail in the pitch darkness. In the black jungle, the light coming from the girl's flashlight seems small.

The daughter walks fast. She takes short-cuts through the fields. She is unafraid. But the animals are terrified as lightning zigzags through the sky. Horses gallop through the fields, whinnying, their thundering hooves shake the earth.

The jungle and the fields are alive with shrieks and cries of animals and birds as the girl follows the daughter to the house of the man by the lagoon.

The man lives in a two-room shack with his family. He is very poor. When they reach the shack, the daughter calls out. A child comes and opens the wooden gate. It's beginning to rain hard again. The child leads them into the room. It is pitch black like the jungle. They have no lights, not even candles. The girl turns her flashlight on the children. There are six of them in thin ragged clothes. The mother comes in from the kitchen which is pitch black too. Her husband isn't back yet, she says. They will have to wait.

The children look at the flashlight. They have never seen a flashlight before. The girl turns it on and off. The more she turns it on and off, the more the children laugh. Laughing, they take it from her hands, they shine it in each other's eyes.

Then the girl takes the flashlight back. With fast sweeping strokes, she paints patterns of light in the air. In awe, the children watch, their eyes wide. The girl repeats the strokes over and over. When she stops, the children clap their hands and scream for more.

The girl puts the flashlight in her pocket while the children scream for more. She covers her ears to muffle their screams. She closes her eyes. In a dream, she sees the sky, the bright blue sky. She is standing under the bright blue sky at the edge of the lagoon. There is wind. She is about to rise with the wind into the bright blue sky when she looks at the water. She sees the floating plants. She sees the water lilies with flat green leaves. She sees the insects skating on the surface. In the dream, she changes her mind and chooses the water. Something inside her wants the water, needs the water in the dream more than the bright blue sky.

She goes into the water. The water is dark with life. Thick with life. She can barely see into it as she goes through the water, her feet padding along the bottom. The soft and muddy bottom. She goes down, all the way down in the water. When she comes up, there are birds all around her: large birds, small birds, birds with hooked bills, birds with broad wings, birds rolling and turning in the air.

She is alive like the birds as she lies on her back, drifting in the dark water of the dream. While she drifts, she spreads out in the water. She is dark and lustrous and waving like the water. She is large like the water. Getting larger. She is losing the boundaries of the body. The water is taking over the body. The water is making over the body. The body is no longer a body. The body is all over the water. It is the light playing on the surface. It is the darkness. It is where birds plunge, where fish swim, where frogs and insects lay their eggs. Worms and snails and crayfish live in its depths. The body is no longer separate from the water. That wanting to get out of the body, that wanting to be water is what she was and what she will be again. But for a little while, there is only water. The wanting is only water.

ABOUT THE AUTHOR

Roberta Allen is the author of two collections of short fiction, *The Traveling Woman* (Vehicle Editions, 1986, Painted Leaf Press, 2000) and *Certain People* (Coffee House Press, 1997); a novella in short short stories, *The Daughter* (Autonomedia, 1992); a memoir, *Amazon Dream* (City Lights, 1993); the writing guide, *Fast Fiction: Creating Fiction In Five Minutes* (Story Press, 1997); and the novel, *The Dreaming Girl* (Painted Leaf Press, 2000). Allen is on the faculty of The New School, and has taught at Columbia University. She was a Tennessee Williams Fellow in 1998. Her articles have appeared in *The Sophisticated Traveler* of *The New York Times,* and other publications. She is an established visual artist who has exhibited worldwide, with work in the collection of The Metropolitan Museum of Art.

Photo © Elizabeth Schub